The revolutionary new approach to
parenting your infant

THE SELF-CALMED BABY

- How overstimulation and your own anxiety can trigger tantrums

- Why breast-feeding is a sexual issue and a feeding question

- Tips on teething, birthmarks, umbilical cord care, jaundice, rashes

- How to read babies who don't cry

- What to expect after the hospital

- Help your baby develop social skills and self-control using hand-sucking, vision, changing position, rocking

- Create a calming environment for your child

- Why babies who can sleep amid crowds and noise may not really be sleeping at all!

WILLIAM SAMMONS, M.D. is a graduate of Williams College. He developed his theory that any child can learn to self-calm during his residency at Massachusetts General Hospital and a fellowship at Children's Hospital in Boston under renowned pediatrician T. Berry Brazelton, M.D. He further refined his theory in his current private practice in Wellesley, Massachusetts, and in parenting his son.

The Self-Calmed Baby

A Liberating New Approach
to Parenting Your Infant

WILLIAM A.H. SAMMONS, M.D.

WITH A FOREWORD BY
T. BERRY BRAZELTON, M.D.

SMP
ST. MARTIN'S PAPERBACKS

Published by arrangement with Little, Brown

THE SELF-CALMED BABY

Copyright © 1989 by William A. H. Sammons, M.D.

Cover photograph supplied by FPG International.

Library of Congress Catalog Card Number: 88-8322

ISBN: 0-312-92468-2

Printed in the United States of America

Little, Brown hardcover edition/February 1989
St. Martin's Paperbacks edition/April 1991

10   9   8   7   6   5   4   3   2   1

To T. Berry Brazelton and Catherine Morrison, who taught me how to see and hear but most of all to understand

Contents

Foreword

Learning how to become the parent of a new baby is a tense, often overwhelming job. The more a parent cares, the more difficult it may seem. For most new parents, it is a matter of learning from small failures rather than from successes. In the initial period of learning, it is certainly a help to know that most babies are more competent than they appear to be. One of the major breakthroughs of the past few decades is our rapidly increasing knowledge of the competencies of the newborn. I find that this knowledge is a real support for new parents. Their concern for not damaging or neglecting their new baby makes them more aware of their own inevitable stress and depression after they bring a new baby home. Learning to see him* as competent to communicate his needs to them is a real relief. They can dare to learn his "language." His behavior and his behavioral responses are indeed his language, as verbal language is for adults.

The Self-Calmed Baby teaches parents how to observe.

---

* For simplicity's sake, although I deplore the sexism this reinforces, I shall use the masculine pronoun for the baby and the feminine pronoun for the parent.

With its excellent descriptions of infant responses over the first few critical weeks, it gives parents the information they need to learn this language. It also gives them permission to dare to trust their own eyes and their baby's competencies. The practical advice that is offered to parents as they come home from the hospital is especially helpful. A new baby presents an opportunity for a major readjustment of the whole family. If the parents can shut out the demands of the rest of the world at such a time, they can "become a family." This is a time for being nurtured by the extended family, but not for meeting unnecessary demands. It is a time to conserve all energy in order to learn the new job of nurturing and adjusting to this new individual. Dr. Sammons's advice will help parents make these decisions.

Learning how to observe and communicate with the new baby is the major task of the postpartum period. In *The Self-Calmed Baby*, Dr. Sammons describes the complexity of the newborn's communications. He points out that, in one's urgent desire to be a good parent, one can all too unwittingly overwhelm and disorganize the baby's raw nervous system. Learning his different behavioral patterns, learning to differentiate his many different cries, can enrich and speed up the process of becoming a parent. This book will aid enormously in that process.

When a parent learns to observe and use her baby's behavior as the base for her responses to him, she is learning to respect him. With this respect, she will pass on a sense of competence to him. In his excellent analysis of crying behaviors, Dr. Sammons gives parents an opportunity to learn to differentiate between the cries that need intervention and those that can be handled by the infant himself. His concept of teaching the baby to learn to self-calm is an important insight for families. Babies can learn behavioral patterns that serve them when they are overloaded and disintegrating. Too much parental input only overloads the baby even further. Crying at the end of the day, which starts out as a discharge of an overloaded nervous system, becomes "colic" when frantic parents add their tension to the baby and, through their extra attention, add stimuli that he can no longer handle at the end of the day. Learning to pull back, observe, and to give the baby credit for behavioral competencies to learn the self-calming techniques Dr. Sammons advocates becomes a breakthrough for new parents. Their respect for the baby increases, and their own ability to observe and to trust their observations increases their own self-competence. This, then, can become a powerful addition to a sense of trust in the parent-infant attachment process. It does not mean that they will desert him or leave him to learn these patterns alone. The job for parents is to learn the fine line between when to intervene and when to leave the baby to find his own competent behavioral pattern of self-calming. Dr. Sammons tells parents how to support the baby as he learns.

This, then, leads to learning about mastery — mastery on the new parents' parts to allow the baby to learn to calm himself, and the reinforcing of mastery in the baby. For the infant, the task is that of learning how to bring himself out of a fussy, crying state into one over which he has control. Dr. Sammons gives new parents a unique, important window into the behavioral processes involved in early infancy, which can be captured as parents endeavor to "teach" children self-reliance and self-calming. When this effort works, it will reinforce children with a necessary sense of competence.

My only concern is that parents see self-calming as a way to become more involved with their child, not less. Dr. Sammons shares my concern that parents not leave the child too much to his own devices, however powerful and important, in infancy, and that they provide a constant environment of nurturing and sensitivity to the infant's cues. I'm not sure whether insecure parents (and we all are) can decide easily about this balance. The specific guidelines in *The Self-Calmed Baby* are a great help toward this important effort. Parents must still make their own decisions about when and how they should respond and when it is time to turn the controls back to the baby. This book will surely help them learn to make the right decisions for their family.

In this light, "Parents have influence but they don't have control" is an insight that may both comfort and unsettle new parents. By way of comforting them, it points to the fact that the baby makes his own major contribution and that he is competent to make an impact on his own outcome. Parents who want to learn to respect their baby's behavioral language will find this book invaluable. Trusting him to learn early, effective self-calming techniques will reinforce their sense of his contribution. Their own need to nurture him and to learn their task of adjusting to their new role, however, can unsettle them. Dr. Sammons warns that their

efforts to control the baby's behavior can all too easily
lead to patterns of overstimulation or overprotection.
The Self-Calmed Baby gives new parents unique ideas
about how to draw this fine line in deciding when to
intervene and how to measure their own success by
observing the baby's responses to them. When parents
become adept at this important but difficult task in infancy, it may help in later stressful periods in the child's
development, such as adolescence. In my experience,
learning to separate and to give the child critical independence may well be the most difficult job in parenting. If a parent knows how to use the baby's reactions
to make these decisions, she will be ready to trust the
child's autonomy at each new stage of development.
This is a lifetime learning process — for the parent and
for the child. This wonderful book will be an important
aid in the learning, hopefully, for all parents.

T. BERRY BRAZELTON

Acknowledgments

This book is only partly mine. It would not exist without the parents and patients in my practice. The doctors I cover with, especially Dr. Paula Curran, and my office staff, Kate Tonner and Ginny O'Malley, also deserve credit; without them I would have had no time to write.

Helen Rees, my agent, had the patience to stick with this project, and the ideas and thoughts became readable only with the help of Wendy Murphy and the editing of Jennifer Josephy and her assistant, Sarah Pence, at Little, Brown.

My mother deserves special credit for putting up with my eighteen months of colic when many others would have thrown out the baby with the bath water.

Kathy DiPilato is indispensable in more ways than I can say.

And finally, there are the people who literally gave up so much while making sure that I was able to write this book: Marilyn, Mikko, Red, Carol, and the genius who's always there on top of the CRT providing inspiration at 2 A.M., Albert.

Author's Note

In any book for parents the use of she and he is always a problem. Since not all parents are mothers and not all babies are sons, I have varied the gender to include fathers and daughters.

All the stories in this book are true. The names and identities have all been changed, but the words and feelings have not.

I have started a nonprofit group called Red Tae Associates to help parents who have concerns about their children's development. If you have questions about self-calming or how it can be used with older children to work out problems with sleep, discipline, or sibling relationships, please call me at 800-422-6661.

The Self-Calmed Baby

Introduction

My fascination with child development began in medical school. Although originally my goal was to become a specialist in adult intensive care medicine, early in the second year I discovered the world of children's growth and development. I knew then that my career would be in pediatrics. Six years later, I finished my residency having acquired vast amounts of knowledge and having read many shelves of books. Yet I still felt dissatisfied.

Many of my observations about babies did not seem to match with what I had been told. Some things, in fact, didn't make sense at all. I constantly wondered why, among the hundreds of sick and healthy babies I saw, some appeared to have a much easier time adjusting to life than others. It seemed to me that parents and doctors were failing to notice something about these children that would explain the differences. I made it my goal to figure out what that missing piece of information was.

Little that I heard in medical school or residency was much help in understanding what the mysterious ingredient might be. Babies were presented as rather primitive organisms, physically intact, but whose sensory, mental, and emotional development had yet to take place. Just like parents now, we were taught to think of infants as wholly helpless and incompetent, their psychological development almost totally dependent on the adults around them. Even today, despite all the discoveries that have been made about neonatal hearing, sight, sensation, and cognition, many pediatricians still find the idea of a two-month-old being able to self-calm difficult to accept.

Fortunately, after residency I had the opportunity to spend two years studying with Dr. T. Berry Brazelton, a professor of pediatrics at Harvard Medical School and one of the most original, creative, and insightful leaders in the field of child behavior and development.

Dr. Brazelton encouraged me to take a different look at children. He wanted me to see what infants and toddlers *could* do, not what they could not do, which was an approach distinctly different from what I had met in all my previous years of studying child psychology and medicine. I came to see that the development of each child is not locked into some timetable of achievements that can be memorized. Each child has great potential and startling competence, even as a newborn, and each is distinctly his own person with his own timetables. I was shocked out of my ignorance. But I still had to learn.

Although Dr. Brazelton encouraged me to stay in academic medicine and developmental research, I decided to go into practice on the theory that it would be the best environment for learning more about infants and children. The choice has proved to be even more fulfilling than I dreamed possible. In some ways, being a practicing pediatrician is like raising hundreds of kids at once. Each child puts a singular twist on life, and my practice has offered me a unique view of both the amazing competencies of children and the many different ways there are to be a parent.

Unfortunately, most parents have taken their first training for parenthood by reading books that are woefully out of step with current knowledge. When we first meet, they arrive with expectations born of reading abbreviated versions of the same developmental timetables that I was given back in medical school. They know all about what to look for in motor development: the baby discovers her hands in the second month; the baby can sit propped up in the fifth or sixth month, and so on. But they are not encouraged to see how competent their child is. She has other, more exciting capabilities, especially the ability to self-calm.

Lacking this knowledge, it is hardly surprising that most parents are overprotective and controlling or that most children must win whatever independence they can at the price of a struggle. How much more joyous and fulfilling it would be for everyone were each child encouraged and supported in his efforts to mature at his own rate, according to his genuine abilities. Helping parents and their children to understand each other better, to communicate more successfully, are among the foremost goals of my practice and of this book. Today's busy parents, who need to make the most of every moment they have with their children, really cannot afford to do otherwise.

As a new pediatrician, I was in much the same position as many of these parents. But I did not yet see what I needed to know. I hadn't found the missing information I was seeking. Only by listening to parents in my practice, especially those whose children had colic, did I finally discover the missing piece of the puzzle: self-calming.

Colic, as much as sleep, eating, or discipline problems was important to me because I identified personally with difficult babies. My mother tells me that I had colic for the first eighteen months of my life — probably a world record! Constant nursing, near-toxic doses of paregoric and bananas, and endless hours of holding, rocking, and walking by every member of the family had failed to make a dent in my frantic behavior. No one could soothe me, and I could not calm myself.

I now realize that the first inkling I had that babies could self-calm and that it might have some value to them was when I worked with premature infants in the Neonatal Intensive Care Unit (NICU) at Massachusetts General Hospital. This was an extremely demanding environment for children, parents, and medical staff alike because of each baby's critical health status. Everyone was under constant tension, in surroundings that featured bright, twenty-four-hour-a-day fluorescent lights and intense, unremitting, and unsettling noises. The necessary medical procedures often involved a great deal of physical pain for the child and emotional pain for the parents; it was very rare that anyone could take the time to consider the individual personality or the feelings of the tiny patient. But as I helped care for them, I noticed that those infants who sucked on their hands or on their feeding tubes — or even their endotracheal tubes — seemed to have fewer medical problems, as though they were somehow more resilient. I also began to realize that the adults involved, including parents, nurses, physicians, and technicians, who could best buffer themselves from the stress held up under the tension better and were less likely to "burn out" or become emotionally and physically exhausted.

Initially, I didn't think of the behavior I'd seen in the NICU as "self-calming." Indeed, I first heard the term some years later during my fellowship with Dr. Brazelton. It was one of dozens of items on the Brazelton Newborn Assessment Scale designed to assess newborn behavior. But the idea and its implications for adults were familiar.

Earlier in my training I had worked personally and professionally with family therapists who used techniques derived from meditation and Eastern religion to help adults achieve greater self-control. In my work with these therapists, especially Catherine Morrison, I began to see how much stress I needlessly endured because I didn't have better self-calming skills. In trying to understand infants, I needed to look no further than my own reactions and emotions. I started to regard self-calming not as one of many developmental achievements but as probably the most important one. It seemed to me that self-calming could help anyone — a premature infant, a newborn baby, or an adult — be more in control of his own life. But how did the baby arrive at this skill and what could parents do to help the process?

As a new pediatrician, I didn't dare try the concept

in my practice without solid evidence to support it. So I continued to listen sympathetically to parents' painful stories of crying babies, feeling helpless to make things better for them. I did not understand what the behavior meant and I certainly had no advice that was likely to produce a rapid improvement in their situation. All I did know was that none of the traditional drugs, changes in diet for nursing mothers, nor any of the other "cures" commonly recommended for colic — for example, switching to a different formula or constant holding of the baby, or both, really worked. Occasionally, when in desperation I would suggest one of these standard remedies, the poor results would only make me more appreciative of the hell my mother had gone through with me.

As my practice grew and I saw more and more families, colic seemed to me as significant a family crisis as separation anxiety and the "terrible twos." In fact, I suspected that one led to the other. It seemed that no matter what parents did, something else was needed to get everyone through it.

One afternoon it happened that my schedule included six appointments with infants one or two months old. Each set of parents had called in the days just preceding. Each family was in crisis as a result of seemingly endless crying and no sleep. Nothing so far had helped. Indeed, the more suggestions they tried, whether from books, grandparents, or friends, the worse it all got. Everyone wanted new and better suggestions, and I didn't have any. I felt pushed to the wall. How many times could I let parents endure this unhappiness? I decided to gamble on the radical new approach that I'd been thinking about for months. I wasn't going to cure these children, and neither were the parents going to cure them. With the parents' cooperation, each baby was going to help herself.

The decision felt like a very big risk. My practice was still relatively small but growing. By doing something unorthodox, I could lose all my patients and find myself back at square one. In order to succeed, I had to convince parents that their children were capable of doing something that no other pediatrician and no parenting book had ever said was possible. As each appointment unfolded, I explained my concept to the parents and talked about the ways I thought that they could help the agitated and "colicky" child. I asked each family to call me when they had something to report or if there were other questions.

I went home that night worried about what would happen. At 2 A.M. I was staring at the ceiling — one moment convinced that I was right, the next moment fearing I wouldn't be able to pay the mortgage if I was wrong. Fortunately, within two days I knew the answer. Each of the six couples had seen a change for the better. By the end of the week, parents were calling to say they felt as though they were living with a different child. Not only was there less crying, but the parents could say exactly why the crying had stopped. Each family was happier, sleeping better, but no two babies were doing exactly the same thing to calm themselves.

Even I was amazed at the effect of self-calming and intrigued by the individual expression and variation in each child. New ideas and new suggestions occurred in an avalanche — at least as many coming as suggestions from parents as from my own observations of each baby I saw. Because of its effectiveness, even with older children, self-calming became the central focus of my advice for parents. Word of mouth soon made a small practice a booming success. Self-calming was no longer just a radical, untested theory. It was beginning to look like fact!

And what has happened since? Well, I have come to see that self-calming is a skill system that consists of a number of techniques that the child who is crying or disorganized can use to settle himself down and/or stop crying *entirely on his own*. It means that parents do *not* have to walk, talk with, rock, or feed the baby; they do not have to give the baby a pacifier or a "lovey" or intervene in any other way.

How does the baby self-calm? Infants have many skills that they use to self-calm. Babies use sucking (yours may use her wrist), movement of their hands, arms, or legs (yours may use hand motions in front of her face), a certain body position (yours may like her left side better than any other position), or vision (yours may focus on a light, a window, or a white wall). As they get older, children develop many other motor skills and social behaviors and, eventually, use language as a way to self-calm.

How long does this take to develop? There is no specific timetable, but there is a predictable sequence of events as a child masters each skill. Most infants are making attempts to self-calm in the first weeks; just about all have some success by eight to ten weeks. What your baby chooses to do and how soon the baby succeeds depends on how you work together — self-calming is a mutual achievement. It requires that you give up a number of popular myths and fantasies about children, that you and the baby make certain decisions and set specific priorities that maintain each person's autonomy. These include helping the baby by managing a smooth transition home from the hospital, establishing an effective communication system between you and your child, and, especially, learning the meaning of different cries.

What does self-calming mean to the baby? Why does the baby want to participate? Parents say over and over again that self-calming made their child happier, more social, and more fun. Self-calming is indispensable for the baby, who can now cope with the ups and downs of the world, the thousands of unexpected happenings that occur every day. The sudden noise that used to startle him and make him cry may still startle him, but he turns, looks out the window, gets settled down, and does not cry. Tired and disorganized, he used to fuss and cry when you put him to bed, now he simply sucks on his hand to go to sleep. Long before he has developed other skills like crawling, walking, or talking, self-calming allows the child to build self-esteem and self-confidence by letting him feel he has some control over the world.

As he gets older, self-calming is the means for increasing self-sufficiency and independence. Unless he has the basic skills to self-calm and keep his behavior organized, he cannot gain self-control or entertain himself.

What does self-calming mean to parents and the family? Once the baby can self-calm, she has independent ways to cope and is no longer so dependent on her parents. Self-calming secures autonomy for you and your baby. This makes going back to work, using baby-sitters, taking a vacation, maintaining a relationship with your spouse, your other children, and your friends easier and more enjoyable.

Nine years after that fateful afternoon, I continue to define and improve the concept and to learn new ways that children can make use of self-calming. It is the missing piece in the puzzle — your child's most important developmental skill.

CHAPTER 1

The Test: Colic

"He's yours, for free. In fact, we'll pay you to take him,"
Peter Hooper said gruffly, thrusting his crying, struggling five-week-old son toward me. Arm's length was
evidently the only safe distance with Timothy. I could
see from the milk stains on his father's shirt and all
over his mother's dress that Timmy spat up often and
in large amounts.

Sandi, his wife, forced a smile, but neither of the
Hoopers laughed. I was meeting them for the first time.
They looked much like any other parents who have
been struggling with a new baby — tired, anxious,
frustrated, desperate for an answer to one question,
"How do I make this livable?" I glanced at their four-
year-old, who was gazing out the window. What did
Erin think of this new baby? Was she mad at him or
did she feel sorry for his apparent suffering?

The Hoopers had been referred by Pam Duncan,
whose own child was a patient of mine. She had convinced Peter and Sandi that her baby, now thriving after
a difficult start, had been a lot like Timmy in the beginning. She urged them to see me and, near desperation,

they had decided to take her advice even though it meant driving forty-five minutes to get to my office.

Our appointment was at five o'clock — what I like to call the "arsenic hour." Like many infants at that time of day, Timothy couldn't stop crying. His wailing was so loud that it made conversation difficult even in other parts of the office and almost impossible in his company. But that was the whole point of scheduling the appointment at that time — I wanted to see Timmy at his worst.

"Like you," I began, "a lot of parents spend the first months wondering why they ever wanted to have a baby. The family that just left here felt exactly the same way a couple of months ago. They were convinced that their son had something wrong with his stomach, or that he was suffering from the world's worst case of colic. Now Ryan is fine. Like Timothy, like most five-week-old babies, Ryan needed to learn how to self-calm."

Sandi raised a skeptical eyebrow. I continued. "You know what you've seen Pam Duncan's children do; that's why you drove all this way. We'll find ways that will enable Timmy to calm himself and stop crying without your having to nurse him, rock him, walk him, or do anything else. By sucking on his hand, or using vision, or perhaps a certain body position, Timmy will self-calm and he won't need your help, or Peter's, or Erin's."

Sandi's skepticism was now mixed with a little curiosity and hope. "Sounds like a great idea, but I don't think it is possible. Just because it worked for Pam doesn't mean it will work for us. She started seeing you right away — are we too late?" She reached over to take Timmy. "Maybe he's hungry." Her downcast eyes and her tone of voice showed little hope that nursing would solve the problem, but she gave it a brave try. Timmy squirmed and turned away first from one breast and then the other. He scrunched his eyelids closed, clenched his fists, and let out a piercing screech. Erin held her hands over her ears. I wondered how much Timmy would choose to block out if only he could cover his ears.

Peter glared at Timothy, and then me, his face hollow with fatigue. I was sure that he had been up all night, probably for many nights in a row. "Our life is falling apart. Modern medicine had better have something to help us, or I hate to think where we'll be after a few more weeks of this."

During the next twenty minutes I listened while the Hoopers poured out a tale of disruption, disappointment, and discord. Peter, a cabinetmaker, and Sandi, a legal secretary, had looked forward to Timmy's birth with great anticipation. They had had fun with Erin, except that they remembered the newborn period was a struggle. So Sandi had arranged to take two months off from work and Peter had cut back his work schedule so that he would have more free time at home to get to know Timmy. Nevertheless, life had been a nightmare ever since. Time alone wasn't enough.

"Last night I thought that we were headed for divorce court." Peter reached over to take his wife's hand. He was half smiling, and I wondered why.

Sandi, somewhere between crying and laughing, explained. "It turned out that we were both having the same fantasy — about having an affair and running away. But not from each other — from Timmy!"

Peter concurred. "It's amazing the havoc a tiny little baby can wreak on a happy marriage. I'm beginning to doubt whether the kid is really worth the trouble."

Listening to Sandi and Peter, there was no question that Timothy had made a chaos of their lives. He reportedly slept all day and was up all night, most of it spent crying. After five weeks of this, Peter and Sandi were at the end of their respective ropes, and they were worried about Erin. There was no consistent feeding schedule. Each nursing was a battle. Sandi's nipples were cracked and bleeding. Despite days of constant feeding, she was worried that Timmy wasn't getting enough to eat. As we talked, they shuttled Timmy back and forth between them, with no discernible effect on his state of being. Not once did he stop his crying, or worse, that awful shrieking.

As the Hoopers sought to assure me, they had followed up every bit of helpful advice from well-meaning relatives, in-laws, and friends about how to make Timmy happy. Long before he was born, not wanting to rely on their memory from four years ago with Erin, they had done their prospective-parent homework thoroughly, attending a six-week prenatal course and a class on breast-feeding. They had read three popular books on child care, all but memorizing the chapters on newborns. Since Timmy's birth they had been to see two other pediatricians in search of solutions. Nothing had made the reality of Timmy any better.

"All our in-laws do is pour salt in the wound. I'm going to kill Peter's mother right after my own if either one of them tells me one more time that Timothy's problem is colic and that everything will be fine if I will just give him formula or stuff him with bananas." She hesitated briefly, and then confessed, "On the other hand, I'm so desperate that I thought about it last night, although I could never tell my friends in the nursing mothers group."

Sandi reached over to take Timmy, who chose that moment to spit up on his father. Desperately trying to find some humor in the situation, Peter reached for a Kleenex. "Keep it up and you'll wear out the washer and dryer. Maybe the dry cleaner will give him a commission."

Timothy's shrieking was so intense that I wondered for a moment if perhaps there *was* something wrong with his stomach after all. But Timothy would feed perfectly at 2 A.M. He did not have diarrhea or any other signs of intestinal problems. And clearly Timmy was getting enough to eat — he was huge. Experience told me that an infinitely more likely cause for his misery was overstimulation. My guess was that Timmy was suffering, too, from the effects of his parents' feelings of anxiety, frustration, and exhaustion, and that he was behaving in ways that inevitably fueled the problem. If I was right, Sandi and Peter could change things around, but they could only do so with Timmy's cooperation. That was where I came in; I could show all of them how to get Timmy started at self-calming. Perhaps that was not exactly what Peter had in mind when he pleaded for "modern medicine," but the techniques involved are as "modern" as our understanding today of how marvelously competent infants really are.

"Why don't you let me have Timmy for a minute," I said, reaching toward the embattled Sandi. As I took the baby, his body stiffened noticeably. His lips were a little bluish, his breathing fast. I held him in front of me, expecting him to vomit. He opened his eyes, looked at me with a mix of horror and surprise, and started to cry again. I thought to myself, Timmy is going to be a tough customer.

Sandi kept trying to talk, but I motioned her to stop. I closed the window shades, turned off the lights, and slowly, gently placed Timothy on his stomach atop the examining table. His wail changed to fussing. That looked like a hopeful sign, but almost immediately he started crying again. I watched for a minute to see if he would try to help himself. Nothing. Hoping to find a position that would calm him, I rolled Timmy onto his back. Next I tried putting him on his right side, facing the shaded window. Briefly his arms and legs stopped flailing, then he gagged. I pushed his hand toward his mouth — maybe he wanted something to suck on. No such luck. I tried swaddling him with his blanket, but that only made things worse. I was fast running out of options. I applied gentle, constant pressure on his back. Nothing. I talked to him in a soft monotone. Again nothing. Something had to work, I reassured myself. Maybe he could use his vision to calm down. It hadn't worked with the window, but I didn't have much choice. I propped him on his left side, his face to the bare white wall, and held my breath. Timothy stared straight ahead, whimpered, and suddenly stopped crying.

I sat down, somewhat relieved. But the motion or

the sound got him going again. Sandi started to go to his rescue, but I waved her back to her seat. Timothy cried for about thirty seconds, repeatedly hitting himself in the face as he tried to get to his hand. It was painful watching him struggle. I hoped he would go back to looking at the wall — the easy way out. But that wasn't Timothy. At last he got his wrist in his mouth. Sucking furiously, he stopped crying but continued squirming. With so much activity, he lost his wrist again. He cried for twenty seconds, and then, with what seemed like an intense effort, he maneuvered his arm back to his mouth and took hold. Finally content, lips smacking loudly, he relaxed.

The entire drama from start to finish had taken five minutes, but it seemed like an eternity. Even now, if we raised our voices above a whisper, Timothy would start to cry again. As soon as we were quiet, he would find his hand again.

Relaxed, Peter and Sandi slumped in their chairs. "That's the first time he's ever done that," Peter said as Sandi nodded her head in wonderment. For a moment, we simply sat without speaking, not wanting to disturb the nice, even cadence of Timmy's sucking. Finally, Peter leaned forward and whispered the million-dollar question: "How do we get him to do this at home?"

I startled them when I said, "You don't *get* him to do it. That is Timmy's responsibility. We'll talk about the ways that you can help him, but he is the one who must learn to self-calm."

Fortunately, the Hoopers were all quick learners. Even Erin found ways to help out. Four days after our first meeting, Sandi called to report back that Timmy had changed for the better, not just a little, but a lot. Three weeks later, I was able to confirm the progress myself when I saw them for their second appointment. Timmy was happily, quietly bouncing on his father's lap. Erin got a smile and a squeal of delight from him. Sandi was noticeably more confident and relaxed. She made the appropriate observation: "Everyone paints such a rosy picture; it's deceiving. I wish they told you the truth about what living with a newborn is really like."

The Hoopers' experience is, in a sense, the inspiration for this book. With each newborn, every parent faces unanticipated changes and new decisions, and it makes no difference whether both parents have careers or one stays home to care for the baby. As a pediatrician, one of my goals is to help families avoid the kind of crisis of adjustment that the Hoopers went through. Such parents miss out on much of the excitement and fun of the initial weeks because they do not understand the limits of their power as parents. Parents have influence, but they do not have total control. Nor are they always fully aware of their baby's potential. As a result, their child is kept in a helpless state. Until the baby learns to self-calm they go through an extended nightmare of missed sleep, guilty thoughts, anxiety, marital battles, and endless conflicts with in-laws, friends, and employers. Mothers yearn to go back to work. Fathers worry that they have no relationship with their baby, even as they feel guilty about fleeing the house each day to go to the relative peace and quiet of their jobs. Both parents think wistfully of the freedom they used to have before the pregnancy and of the hours of undisturbed sleep they once enjoyed.

The key to putting everyone on a firmer foundation lies in the way we think about newborns. In the last twenty years babies finally have been recognized as the human beings they are rather than the passive, blank slates they were once thought to be. From the moment of birth, a baby can see and hear and think. He's an individual, with unique concerns and abilities. Like his parents, the infant is a partner with equal responsibility for creating and sustaining a happy relationship with members of the family. To carry out his part of the bargain, however, he must learn to communicate and to develop clear behavior signals, skills for which he is naturally competent.

Self-calming makes all of this possible. With self-calming the infant is able to assert control over his own reactions to those things or events that used to make him cry or become disorganized. By sucking on his hand, staring out a window, maneuvering into a certain body position, or some other self-calming skill, he can keep himself from crying or stop crying — without help from his parents. Thus he develops an enhanced feeling of security and competence. And the infant's success in self-calming is circular. The calmer the baby, the greater the quantity and quality of time that his parents can spend with him. The more time they spend together, the better their relationship grows, as each becomes more adept at communicating. Then, and only then, do love and attachment grow and flourish.

Not only does self-calming conform to what we know physiologically about the roles of mind-body control and stress reduction in sustaining optimal mental and physical health for the baby, it makes good sense for parents, too. Busy two-career families cannot afford, financially or spiritually, to dedicate a mother or father to full-time care of a baby for months on end. And the parent (or professional caregiver, for that matter) who remains at home all day, cannot take the endless frazzle that living with an out-of-control child entails. No adult ought to neglect self, career, marriage, or mind in the total service of a child at the risk of breeding resentment and unhappiness.

At the same time, I can say confidently that the mothers and fathers I meet in my practice want to be as caring and thorough as any other generation of parents, if not more so. They want to do more than just respond to their child's needs; they want to know why their child behaves in certain ways and how this behavior distinguishes her from other children. They realize that their choices regarding limit-setting and discipline, feeding, sleeping, and how they choose to spend their time are vital to the long-term development of their child.

This book provides new and prospective mothers and fathers with the information and strategies needed to raise psychologically healthy children while still keeping their own mental health. We are only just beginning to see self-calming as the complex skill system it is. The process doesn't just happen; it takes work, and both you and your baby share this mutual achievement.

The next four chapters of this book single out issues that are critical to a new family's survival. The focus is on exploring why self-calming is the child's most important skill. I explain what is really meant by "demand feeding" and answer such important questions as, How should you prepare for discharge from the hospital? Why is nursing a sexual issue as well as a feeding question? Should a father take time off from work after his child's birth, and if so, when is the best time? I discuss the false promises of bonding, natural childbirth, nursing, and maternal instinct. I explain why a new mother, with or without a career, should take time for herself and her marriage, and how doing this from the first day home from the hospital helps the child become more self-sufficient and secure.

Chapters 2 through 5 will help you to understand better the two subsequent chapters on self-calming and will allow you quickly to put these ideas to work. Since self-calming has so much potential and is a new idea, Chapter 6 describes the different ways that babies self-calm and Chapter 7 describes the sequence of events that leads to mastering this skill. There is no set timetable; it may take six weeks, or even months, but the sequence of events is predictable. The final chapter, "Setting a Schedule," is about the practical problems of making self-calming work for your family and outlines the different choices that you and your baby make to help to set a comfortable daily schedule. As the baby becomes adept at self-calming, families may begin to establish a comfort level — a predictable, manageable daily rhythm. In a nutshell, they set a schedule. This usually takes about three months, and the patterns of self-sufficiency that are established here can have lifelong impact.

My ultimate goal is to encourage you to see your child as the unique individual he is and, in knowing him, to help him develop the social skills and self-control necessary to survive comfortably in this world. In doing so, I ignore developmental charts that would tell us when our children should achieve this or that skill. Children of the same age ought not be seen as made from some universal recipe and cut to the same size with the same psychological and developmental cookie cutter, any more than you ought to be measured against the standard of "the average husband" or "the typical wife." There is only you, your child, and your family. These people, not some mythical stereotypes, are whom you need to know as you nurture your relationship into a deeper love.

Growing up is every child's most cherished goal. Witness the little girl who has just celebrated her fourth birthday: when asked her age, she gleefully replies, "Almost five!" proudly holding up a handful of fingers. Chances are, you will watch the process of your own child's growth with a mixture of pride and poignancy, with each birthday being one more milestone on the road to independence, to higher personal ambitions, to wider choices. It can be unsettling if you have imagined your role as parent to be one of all-powerful protector with your child as all-dependent. If you treat her as a competent person you share her achievements rather than being an unwanted spectator. She must become autonomous, and no skill you can help her develop will be more valuable in getting there than the ability to self-calm.

CHAPTER 2

Mythology and Fantasies

*New Perspectives on Pregnancy, Childbirth,
Bonding, and Breast-feeding*

We are limited by what we believe to be the truth. A
generation ago no one could have written a book on
self-calming because everyone thought babies were
blind, deaf, and helpless. Many parents still think that
babies arrive with scarcely any skills. Believing that infants are unable to think or to help themselves, parents
have guaranteed that children waste the great gifts actually in their possession. Today, science and psychology are constantly expanding the horizons of what
newborns can do.

Regrettably, in ridding ourselves of one set of false
assumptions, we seem to have taken on a whole new
set. Like the old misunderstandings, these new articles
of faith pose major obstacles to getting the most enjoyment out of parenting. In the present chapter, I will
look briefly at four different facets of beginning parenthood — pregnancy, natural childbirth, bonding, and
breast-feeding — and the sometimes misguided "truths"
that surround them.

No one of these discussions is intended to tell you everything there is to know on the subject. In discussing each facet you and your spouse will have an opportunity to confront some very important issues, reexamine what you may have already accepted on faith as "the only way to go," and perhaps look around for some other alternatives, if you are so inclined. Remember, as you think about the assumptions and truths currently in vogue, that no matter what you have come to believe, no single decision you make is going to guarantee a perfect bond or shatter your relationship with your baby. Many factors go into building a strong connection with your child. It takes time, work, and perseverance.

Pregnancy: A Turning Point

The first myth about pregnancy is that it is something only the mother can experience, that no one else is involved. The reality, however, is that every member of the family, young or old, male or female, changes in the nine months that it takes the embryo to become a baby. The father, siblings, and sometimes even the grandparents become "emotionally pregnant" as they begin to anticipate the baby's arrival and the new role they will play.

Pregnancy has always had its extended effects on the family, but they are far greater today than ever before. The advent of new roles of men and women as mothers and fathers is surely a key factor. A father is no longer so likely to define himself within the family as the sole breadwinner; his wife is often an equal partner in the couple's economic life. With two careers to maintain, both parents must share responsibility in raising the child from the start. Not surprisingly, with this kind of incentive, many men very much want to become a part of the process at the earliest possible opportunity.

Nowadays, the father-to-be frequently accompanies his pregnant wife to checkups at the obstetrician's office and goes to the pediatrician's office, too, beginning with the prenatal interview. The new medical procedures used to manage a pregnancy give him an opportunity to see, hear, and feel the existence of the child long before birth. He has a chance to hear the fetal heartbeat at the same time that the mother first hears it (around ten to twelve weeks), and he sheds the same tears and shares the same smiles of joy at the sounds of the new life he has helped to create. Long before his wife's body has changed enough to appear pregnant, he knows his child is real because he can actually see a picture of the fetus on the ultrasound. And in countless other ways he and his wife share the identical fears, worries, hopes, and dreams as the weeks and months pass.

Another myth about pregnancy is that it is a finite experience, quite separate from parenthood, with no lasting implications of its own. Quite the opposite. Pregnancy is the first chapter in a continuing story involving much more than the production of a baby. It is a time of growth for the parents as well as for the fetus. What happens during the nine months gestation, be it your first, second, or last pregnancy, will have fundamental effects on your experience as parents of the child. Every day in my practice at least one father or mother will draw some analogy to how they felt or planned during the pregnancy when talking about their two-year-old or their role as a parent.

As I tell prospective mothers and fathers, painting the nursery and organizing the baby's layette have their value in getting you ready for your new role, but don't ignore the intangibles in your eagerness to prepare. People need to spend more time with themselves and their thoughts during this waiting time, to confront the new realities of life in an unhurried manner. Use these months to think about what role you and your mate will play with your child and with each other in a family that is no longer just two people. Think about how you will preserve and strengthen your own self-identity under the stress of the physical, emotional, and financial demands of a child. Learn to be sensitive to the differences between your experiences of pregnancy and those of your mate, while you enjoy sharing the commonalities. Examine your career plans and how they may or may not mesh with your goals as a parent and marriage partner. And start adjusting your mind to constant change and a sense of being out of control — only then can you deal comfortably and competently with the inevitable unanticipated changes in your routine that will occur once the baby is born.

When people tell you (as they did me and my wife, Carol, before our first child was born), "Your whole life will change," believe it. Consider what it means, and do whatever you can to make it a part of the way you think about the future. You will soon come to see for yourself that pregnancy leads to changes not only in how you spend your free time or how you decorate your spare bedroom, but to changes in relationships with friends and family members and how you feel about your spouse.

Single friends and childless couples may no longer want to have dinner together, or they may come closer trying to find out more about the experience. Your mother, or mother-in-law becomes a different person — hopefully understanding and more cooperative but, unfortunately, sometimes less helpful than full of unwanted advice. Many people in the neighborhood who never spoke before make more of an effort to be your friend. Indeed, similar dramatic changes may be going on in your marriage. Men and women discover new drive, achieve career goals, and finish household projects that never seemed possible. There is a new concern for each other's health and security, a new feeling of wanting to live longer. And there may be conflict. How will you pay the bills? Men get jealous of their wives' creativity; women resent their spouse's economic independence. Confronting the new dimensions and aspects of your marriage is a part of pregnancy, and how you talk to each other and settle these questions affect both of you as parents long after pregnancy is only a memory.

Another myth that falsely colors pregnancy is that the fetus is part of the mother's body. Just as fathers used to be spectators waiting in the hall outside the delivery room, mothers would spend nine months getting ready to separate from something that was "part of me." When birth is imagined to involve the loss of part of the body, then it can seem very threatening to a woman's sense of security. Fortunately, we now know that the baby is always a separate being, separate from the moment of conception, and never part of anyone else. True, the fetus and the placenta are physically dependent on her, but always separate. Delivery eases this dependence, often at a time when the mother's mind and body can take no more. Her emotions are dominated by one feeling: "Please stop the waiting and let's get this over with."

Remember Peter and Sandi, whom we met earlier as they were struggling to get their second child, Timmy, to self-calm? They provide an instructive example of how a pregnancy can serve (or in their case fail to serve) a couple in preparing adequately for parenthood. Though their understanding came late, their observations on what proved to be a significant turning point in their family life are no less true.

Speaking of the months just past, Peter said, "I think we got too complacent during this pregnancy. We sensed many changes in our lives and our relationship, but we thought they would lead in the same direction as the first pregnancy. So we were kind of casual about the whole experience, didn't give it the sort of attention we did the first time around. We concentrated too much on the baby and spending time with Erin.

"One very good thing that happened for me," Peter continued, "was going through the amniocentesis procedure with Sandi. I actually saw Timmy when he was scarcely bigger than my finger, and that was long before Sandi began to show. That, and waiting for the amniocentesis results, gave me more of a sense of being pregnant myself than the other time, especially when everything came back OK. We had both been worried about that. Once the baby was something real, no longer just an imaginary image, I found myself wanting to do more to prepare for his arrival. I actually began to think about how to plan things so that I would have more time with the baby later. I was also proud that we were going to have a son."

Sandi interjected, "We felt much closer to each other because Peter was more involved, and that may have been part of why we didn't feel some of the same sexual pressures that we had felt before. We had a different sort of intimacy, and there was less emphasis on struggling with the gymnastics of making love.

"Since Peter was taking more time at home, I also had more latitude about my work and when I would go back to the office afterward. Then this big important job came up right at the end of the pregnancy. We talked about it and both felt that Peter had to take it. Besides, we kidded ourselves that Peter's greater interest in this pregnancy was like credit in the bank.

"But we had forgotten that we were three years older than the last time. And we were certainly much more tired, what with my dripping sinuses and getting up to go to the bathroom two or three times a night and keeping up with a bouncing, three-year-old Erin mornings and evenings. When we decided that Peter should take the job we were blithely assuming that Timmy would be just like his sister. Then when Timmy turned out to be his own unique self, not at all like Erin, neither one of us had the extra energy it took to cope.

Peter had shortened his schedule but he couldn't take more time from work, and I wanted my job back to save my own sanity. We were fighting constantly out of desperation."

Peter was smiling ruefully and shaking his head. "I think you get such a glow, such a charge from discovering you are pregnant that you start to believe you can do anything. The positive feelings are much like the feelings you get right after the baby is born. I think that nature does that to help you get through the rest. If I hadn't felt so good, it would have been hard to endure the sense of distance that we experienced as a couple in the first few months when Sandi didn't feel well and needed to sleep more. But the downside of all this euphoria was that I got overcommitted both at work and in my own personal goals. I wanted to be more successful, more creative. Could I do this new contract, spend time with Erin, and be involved with the pregnancy? Yes, but at a price. That took time away from us as a couple, and when the hard times came there was no margin of extra time or energy or self-confidence that we could use to help each other or to get Timmy comfortable. Everyone was suffering. It wasn't enough to save time after he was born. We needed to pay more attention to each other during the pregnancy."

Sandi interrupted, "Peter has an interesting point about the energy. I didn't have any real problems with the pregnancy, but the vomiting in the first trimester was depressing, and it got harder and harder to do the normal things that we usually do together as I got bigger and bigger. Some days I would be feeling sorry for myself, and I'm sure that that was hard for Peter to live with. But by the fifth month I also had days when I felt like superwoman. We both had more energy, but we put it into our jobs and our other goals, and that left us unprepared. Timmy was going to need more than just energy. He also needed a certain kind of sensitivity on our parts, and we were not expecting that. I'd have to say that coming to grips with that fact has been a turning point for all of us."

The Hoopers are quite right in their analysis of the first weeks with Timmy and how they might have used the months of pregnancy to better advantage. But the mistakes are understandable. Peter and Sandi had taken their firstborn, Erin, as their only model of what a baby was like, and Erin had been a dream child. As we talked further, they realized that Erin had used sucking on her hand to calm herself, even when she was only a few days old. So she never cried much and always had more self-control than her brother. It was only natural for them to expect that Timmy would be easy, too. But he was not easy, and the Hoopers had no readily available strategy for coping with such a different child. In the weeks just after Timmy was born, when the Hoopers were at their least flexible, he sorely tested their decisions about who they were and what they valued in their life together.

Childbirth: A Time of Testing

In the last twenty years the whole process of giving birth has changed, mostly for the better. Classes provide valuable information that makes labor and delivery more comprehensible and less frightening. Fathers have finally been included in the delivery room, and mothers are no longer automatically put to sleep during the second stage of labor, a circumstance that only increases a woman's sense of vulnerability and dependence at a time when she needs all the self-esteem and independence she can muster. Why? Being put to sleep is frightening for anyone. You lose all control, you place your life in the hands of someone else, often a person you met only moments before. And, certainly, facing the unknowns and pain of labor and delivery is less traumatic if you feel competent and ready for the task. General anesthesia takes a woman totally out of the picture. It says that she is not competent to handle this unique female role — delivering a baby. That message lasts long beyond delivery. If she can't handle this, if she can't control her own labor, how will she manage as a mother? Raising a child is a constant challenge that draws on all your resources. As in any relationship, no one is in total control. You succeed when you are competent and there is a balance of control; you can't succeed and you won't be competent if you are out of control.

As the pendulum has swung in the direction of greater active participation by parents, not all of the change is progress. A new myth has been established: that childbirth can be enjoyable, which is to say essentially painless, because the mother remains in total control. As often happens in our society, the new way of thinking has become just as doctrinaire as the old, and the pressures to conform just as great. Giving birth has become

an event with competitive goals. To be judged successful it is no longer enough to come away with a healthy
mother and baby — everything has to go smoothly, with
no drugs, and afterward both parents, but especially
the mother, are supposed to be bright and bouncy, as
if nothing major has occurred. Furthermore, if the
mother has done everything right, if the father has been
a successful labor coach, then the baby is expected to
be responsive and alert and an enthusiastic nurser from
the start. Setting such an ideal as a goal of childbirth
ensures that most participants are going to feel as if
they have failed to some extent, hardly the way to build
self-confidence for the tasks ahead.

The expectation of childbirth without pain is particularly cruel. I tell my patients that if they can do it
without pain, and without pain-relieving drugs, great,
but most women cannot. Labor is not enjoyable. It hurts,
and you cannot always control the pain simply by
breathing exercises. When the pain is unbearable, drugs
can help you and your child to have an easier birth. If
you trust your obstetrician to give drugs appropriately,
then drugs should not be a problem. If you don't trust
the doctor to make that kind of decision with you, then
change physicians. Going beyond your endurance and
becoming totally exhausted is not an acceptable alternative.

The advantages of "natural childbirth" enjoyed popular support in the 1970s, partly in reaction to the excessive use of general anesthesia that had preceded it,
and partly because it had become the trendy thing in
European medical practice. But just because excessive
anesthesia has a negative effect on mother and child

does not mean that the absence of drugs is guaranteed to be a benefit. And as for the European practice of natural childbirth, that had more to do with a shortage of anesthesiologists than with any philosophic or medical posture. A Swedish obstetrician I know says that in his country patients routinely want to have epidural anesthesiology available, should they need it.

Another very false message contained in the contemporary view of childbirth is that parents, especially mothers, can control everything, beginning with labor. Such a message only ensures disappointment. With proper preparation at childbirth classes, you and your partner can certainly make the experience more comfortable. But you cannot delay that next contraction until you are ready, and most women can't use their mind or their muscles to banish the pain. Any mother or father who has been through "pushing" knows that you can temporarily contain the urge to push for a few seconds, or ease the pain of contractions, but you can't stop it. These control messages are important because they are the same balance that you seek with your child. If parents-to-be were told the truth about labor and delivery then their expectations about parenthood might be more realistic. As a parent, you have influence but you don't have total control. A mother can use breathing and the father's support to ease the pain or to resist pushing, but she can't control labor; she can't stop the contractions from coming. Similarly, parents can decide when to put a two-month old in his crib, but they can never make him go to sleep. In both instances the lack of control is exactly the same.

Domenic and Terry DeVito, in contrast to Peter and

Sandi, were actively trying to make their second pregnancy very different from their first. Adam had been born by emergency cesarean section. His umbilical cord was wrapped around his neck and shoulder, so that the fetal monitor showed serious depressions in his heart rate with each contraction. Terry had resisted having the C-section, and Adam had been very stressed during the long hours of pushing that preceded the decision to operate. After the delivery, the baby had spent more than a day in the special care nursery, and it had taken Terry several weeks before she really believed she could have a good relationship with her son. She was afraid that having missed the chance to hold him and nurse him at the outset doomed them both to something less than the perfect mother-child bond she had so eagerly anticipated.

When Domenic and Terry brought Adam in for his three-year checkup, the visit soon turned into a prenatal interview all about the matter of how to manage their second childbirth experience better. Terry still hoped for a vaginal delivery, but she was scared that the second child would be at risk of repeating Adam's difficult birth.

"Adam looks great," I said, with pleasure. "He talks incredibly well for a three-year-old."

Terry nodded and then asked, "Do you think he should stay here while we talk about the delivery?"

"Certainly. Why not? He's probably just as involved as you are in this pregnancy, and if you don't talk with him he'll surely pick up on your anxiety and feel it too."

"OK," Terry agreed, "but I need to talk about the

delivery. I'm not sure what to do. Everybody at home keeps telling me that I should have a vaginal delivery. It's better for the baby."

"I'm not sure you can accept that so flatly," I countered. "You know from your experience with Adam that sometimes things can get complicated. The ultrasound last week shows that the baby is as big as he was. I think that we have to rely on the monitor and how the labor goes, just like the last time. You have to make this decision based on what the experience means to you, not to your friends and family."

"I don't know what I think," Terry said. "Won't I recover faster, and won't my milk come in much sooner if I have a normal delivery? Won't we have more time together?"

Domenic edged forward in his chair. "We've been fighting about this. I suppose I started it. I was furious on the way home from the prenatal class at the hospital last night. The instructors make you feel like there is only one way to do this. But my sister had natural childbirth and bonding, breast-feeding, no drugs, and all the rest, but it didn't keep her from being way off base with her daughter. My niece totally rules the house. She has never slept through the night, she's constantly having temper tantrums, and her parents never go out at night because they're afraid of her reaction. My sister certainly did everything that she was told, but that isn't making her a good parent, and she's certainly not happy. Now I see the same thing happening with us. There is just so much pressure to fall into line that you start to wonder if something is wrong with you when you have other ideas."

Domenic paused to look for Terry's agreement, then shook his head. "The instructors remind me of a bunch of grandmothers. They aren't trying to help us determine the best way for us, they want us to do it their way. I'm worried about natural childbirth for Terry. It seems easier to me if we do the C-section. I don't want to go through the terror of thinking that I might lose both Terry and the baby a second time. If we schedule the C-section ahead of time then we know what will happen, and when."

Terry was pensive. "I have many of those feelings, too. But all of these books say that a vaginal birth is a real high. That you feel so good. That the baby is so much better off."

"I've had a lot of patients who say that it is important," I said, "but many more say that they felt misled by the books and the classes. I don't think that you will enjoy this labor any more than you did the last one."

"True, the pushing was no fun," Terry admitted.

There were some practical points I thought Terry and Domenic should consider in making their decision. "Some mothers are so exhausted from the delivery that they take many days to recover, and most of the new insurance-coverage schemes make you go home on the second day after a vaginal birth, whether you feel ready or not. You have a good relationship with your obstetrician, and you trust her to use pain-relieving drugs only as they are appropriate. Women who are committed to natural childbirth often want to push way beyond their endurance, or the baby's. If pain-relieving drugs are used appropriately then there is little or no effect on the baby. And as for the matter of bonding right after birth, you know from your own experience that most of what you've heard is 'hype.' Just look at how you and Adam get along now. And you certainly never 'bonded' in the delivery room. In thinking about how you are going to deliver this baby, then, keep reminding yourself that one of your goals has to be to recover as quickly as possible. If you go home exhausted, then things will only be harder."

"I follow everything you've said," Terry responded, "but I still feel like a failure because of the C-section last time. And the classes are just making it worse."

"I understand your feeling even though I certainly can't agree with it," I reassured her. "And as for the arguments you hear in favor of vaginal delivery, they don't always hold up on examination. For instance, I'm not sure that your milk will come in any faster with a vaginal delivery. It depends on how much your body goes through and how you react to the hospital. It's so different an environment that many people can't get comfortable in a hospital, so they don't get much milk flow until they get home. I think it's great that you can make this decision about what kind of delivery you want, and that the obstetrician doesn't make it for you. But you are setting yourself up for a failure by trying to control the whole experience when that isn't possible. Adam's birth made you feel like a failure and put pressure on you to succeed at breast-feeding him, which only made you more anxious and the nursing more difficult. It would have been far better all around if you could just have concentrated on the fact that he came out of a risky situation healthy and without any problems."

Domenic concluded the interview on a positive note. "I can remember when we came to the prenatal interview before Adam was born. You told us that one of the most important things for us to do was to get in the most flexible state of mind that we had ever been in. I think if we can do that again, then we can make this decision more easily."

Terry and Domenic ultimately decided to try for a vaginal delivery, but they were prepared emotionally to adjust to a C-section if that was what was needed. Three months later she delivered. Once again the cord was compressed, but labor was very fast. In fact, there was almost no pushing involved, and George, their second son, was just fine from the outset. A few extra whiffs of oxygen and he was screaming lustily, so he was quickly given to his parents. Even so, he continued to fuss a lot, as if the hospital was not the place he wanted to be. Holding him didn't seem to make it any better.

Two days later I asked Terry and Domenic how the experience had felt the second time around.

"I'm glad I got to give birth vaginally, but it was not exactly what I expected. I had forgotten what the pushing was like, and at the delivery I felt like my body was going to split open. I certainly didn't feel in control — I don't really see how you can, because the process is sort of running on its own. I suppose by pushing at the right times I helped the delivery along, but there were a few times when I wanted to just say 'Give me one more minute before the next contraction. Just wait until I get my breath back.' That is the part that you want to control and can't."

Domenic's reaction was somewhat different. "Terry seemed to suffer more with this baby, and she certainly is more exhausted now. Of course I hated to see her get cut open when Adam was born, but this was no picnic either. I just don't think that the classes tell you the truth. One of the reasons we decided not to have the C-section was that we thought Terry would have to go through less physically. Why don't they just tell you that it will hurt and that it is no fun, rather than trying to get you to believe that you're going to enjoy it. When it does hurt you feel angry. Either you think that you failed some way in not preventing your wife's pain or that the baby didn't do what he was supposed to. I'm happy everybody is healthy but I don't like the sense of disappointment. It took a day to realize that I really had helped. I had been what Terry needed during that time, and I shouldn't be angry with myself, but I have a lot of negative feelings about the classes and the books. They told me something that I wanted to believe was true but wasn't."

"We talked about that a lot last night," Terry added. "Domenic is reflecting a lot of what I feel. It was nice to hold George right away, but not because of bonding. Even though I have spent lots more time with him in the last two days than I was able to spend with Adam, I certainly don't know George at all, nor do I love him any differently. He's still reacting to the hospital and being born, and I can see that getting to know him will take just as long as it did with Adam. I guess the biggest benefit in having him with me so much is that I can know with my own eyes that he is healthy, something that I couldn't know for several days with Adam."

Many of the problems for Peter and Sandi, and the mixed feelings that occurred for Terry and Domenic, are a result of discovering that they could not control everything about pregnancy and delivery. Contrary to the messages, direct and indirect, there were finite limits to their abilities to make things happen — or not happen. A far more constructive use of the period of pregnancy and labor would have been to learn to hold themselves accountable for what they could achieve and not for what they could only wish for — what I call the "flexible state of mind."

Even when pregnancy and childbirth go more or less according to wishes, there is no guarantee that you won't feel let down by the events immediately afterward. Terry, for example, said that even though she succeeded in giving birth naturally, George did not turn out to be her idealized newborn. She had hoped for an alert, responsive baby for all her exertions, but George spent his first two days either in a cocoon, sleepy and unresponsive, or fussing inconsolably. Because Terry was convinced that he should have been bright and socially responsive, constantly eager to nurse, she thought that something was wrong with him. And she was disappointed that she didn't have her reward. Fortunately, I was able to reassure Terry and Domenic that George was behaving the way most infants do in the first few days. Labor and delivery is tough on babies, and the world they come into is very different from life in the uterus and probably a big shock. They fuss because they want less light, less noise, and less activity around them. Most babies, like their mothers, just want to sleep for the first forty-eight hours. They aren't being unresponsive; there's nothing wrong. Everyone, including the baby, wants to ease out of the hangover.

The control fantasy is no less deceiving to fathers. Men in our society often live under the delusion that they are more in control than women. So, like Domenic, they anticipate a level of participation that never comes. They often experience a sense of failure when they see their wives suffering despite their active coaching in the labor and delivery rooms. There is also a second disappointment that is equally difficult for men. The experience of being involved as a "labor coach" is not as fulfilling as giving birth, and no amount of wishing can make it so. Being at the birth is certainly far better than not being there, but it's not the same as giving birth yourself. For those who have been led to expect more of coaching than it can ever provide, there is a definite letdown, a sense of being a second-class parent.

Many of the courses and books on childbearing do little to prepare fathers for this or any of the other demands and adjustments of being a father. One father in my practice told me that it was only after his child was born, and he was going over the whole experience in his mind, that he realized why he had been such an ambivalent participant in the classes. The condescending approach of the instructors and many of the mothers-to-be had made him just plain angry. How could he feel fairly treated when he was willing to consider giving up career opportunities to make himself more available for parenting, only to be reminded every Wednesday night for six weeks that he was "someplace that I almost didn't belong, treading on my wife's territory."

Just as including fathers is relatively new, so is this particular kind of anger, but I am hearing it repeated with increasing frequency in my office. If fathers are going to be full-fledged parents, and not part-time fill-ins, then treating them as equals must start early. As another father, Roy, a truck driver, complained to me, he was encountering the same kind of narrow-mindedness in childbirth classes as he had heard among some of his coworkers, only in reverse. He was used to hearing some drivers accuse women of "getting out of line" when they started competing for the same jobs for the same pay, but he hardly expected to hear women, including his own wife, act as though he was getting out of line when he showed a desire to be more involved in the pregnancy and birth. It was particularly galling because they acted this way even while claiming to want fathers to come to the classes.

The best advice I can give to any parents who are thinking about how they will approach childbirth is to set your own goals. Coping with labor and delivery is easier if you are flexible and adaptive and if you communicate your fears, concerns, and expectations to your mate and your obstetrician. When I ask mothers what they think about the experience a day or so after they have come through it, and not two years later, when time has dulled some of the sensations, most women say something like the following: "The next time my goal will be just to have a healthy child with a minimum of pain and suffering for me and the baby."

Bonding: Is It for Real?

Bonding is a concept first described in detail by Marshall Klaus and John Kennell in the early 1970s. The subsequent enthusiasm for this idea — both among doctors and parents — has led to many changes in hospital policies, including increased opportunities for parent participation in deliveries, the acceptance of demand feeding and rooming-in, and more liberal visiting hours for fathers. Every effort is made to bring mother and baby together as soon after birth as possible, with the baby frequently being laid right on the mother's stomach, skin to skin, as the final stage of childbirth — the delivery of the placenta — is completed.

But is bonding really all it's cracked up to be? Does it automatically make you a better parent? Does it guarantee that a good relationship will follow? And what happens if you don't, for whatever reason, form that connection right after birth?

One thing seems clear in the light of all the well-meaning exaggerations about the power of bonding. Parents who do not "bond" with their newborn often endure tremendous anxiety in the days and weeks after their child is delivered. In fact, in my experience no other myth about children and parents is more destructive to the natural process of family development than this one. The good news is that the anxiety is totally ill-founded. Most new parents understand bonding to mean love at first sight. This occurs no more often than romantic love at first sight does for mature adults. And when it does, it is still no guarantee that a good relationship will follow.

What then is the sensation that people term bonding? I would call it well-justified elation at having successfully completed one of the most demanding tasks in life, pregnancy and childbirth, and then being presented with a responsive, alert, healthy, intact baby whose perfection often exceeds the parents' wildest expectations. But feeling thrilled, or even just wonderfully relieved, is not to be construed as forming a permanent bond with your baby on the delivery table, as some would have you believe. There is no evidence that the baby has any particular sensation at all, except shock at being expelled from the womb. Everyone is definitely in an altered state — for instance, the only thing that parents want to hear in the delivery room is the baby crying. (Now, how long does that last?) The moments after birth can be thrilling. Enjoy it. You should feel good — about yourself and the baby. But the haggard, exhausted expression on the face of the parent of the eight-week-old who constantly cries because he cannot self-calm tells me that there is no magic epoxy that instantly bonds mother and child together.

I wish the concept were true. How nice it would be to become linked so easily. But in the years since the original data were gathered, studies have failed to replicate the same results. Certainly much of the animal data suggests that this is an important time for the young animal, who actually "imprints" an image of its mother. This permanent impression then influences all of its behavior. But there is no data to show that parents imprint on the young, and nobody currently suggests that human babies imprint on the first adult they see. If they did, then obstetricians would have very large families!

Love at first sight is a one-way process. But it takes two people to make a relationship, which is based on individuals understanding each other and accommodating each other's strengths and weaknesses. That often takes weeks and even months to establish, in a process called attachment. Attachment is complex. Unlike love at first sight, it endures despite disappointment or the difficult realization that no one is perfect — even your own child. Attachment does not depend on a magic moment. If spending time with your baby and holding her in the delivery room makes you feel as if you know more about your child, great! But I want to say as firmly as I can that many parents never have the chance to do this in the beginning, and they still do a stellar job at raising their children. Clinging to a fantasy of instant bonding only wastes energy that parents could better use to strengthen a real relationship. It is far more important to love the child after three months, not three minutes.

Breast-Feeding: For Whose Sake?

For years breast-feeding was out of fashion. Now, it seems, it's the only thing to do. Who can resist the myth that mother's milk is almost as good an insurance policy for a great relationship as bonding? But where again is the hard evidence to show that breast-feeding is unqualifiedly better than the bottle? Yes, in certain situations there may be nutritional advantages or partial protection from particular types of infection. It does establish a different role for the mother. But these must be weighed against the greater convenience and personal comfort some mothers enjoy in bottle-feeding, or the greater sense of involvement that many fathers feel in being able to share in feeding their baby.

I tell parents that choosing how to feed the baby is one of the first decisions that parents can make together, and I urge them to consider the pros and cons carefully, with an open mind, well before the baby is due. It is one of the main topics we discuss in our pre-natal interviews, and I find that mothers, and fathers, too, are likely to struggle mightily over this issue. Take Nancy, for example.

Nancy came to see me in the process of interviewing several pediatricians before her first child was born. Highly organized, she came to the appointment with a list of written questions that she intended to ask, but I sensed that she was uncertain as to what she really wanted to talk about. During a long pause, I asked her how she was going to feed the baby.

She seemed to relax a little as she answered. "I have thought about that for a while. I would like to try breast-feeding, but I don't know if it is worth it. I have to go back to work in six weeks. I suppose I would only be just getting the hang of it before I had to stop. But I have two other friends who are pregnant who talk about nursing as if it's the most important thing they will do. I feel ashamed and a little abnormal that I don't have the same kind of strong feelings about it."

Arlene, also in for a prenatal interview, took a different view. She knew her agenda and she didn't need a list to get to the point. With an expression of grim determination, and perhaps a little fear, she asked how many people in my practice had breast-fed. I was happy to answer her that greater than 95 percent had done so for a significant amount of time, generally at least six months. She asked me if I believed in it, and I said I wasn't sure what she meant by "believed."

I went on to explain that if the decision was only about feeding, then the question about "believing" in it would not be so complicated. But feeding is more a social occasion than an issue of what to eat or when. Parents may be concerned about how much or what a child eats, but the child, whether she's two days, two weeks, two months, or two years old values the social interaction more than the food. Understanding that helps parents make more rational decisions for themselves. Arlene knew all of the ostensible reasons to breast-feed. Nursing was worth it to her, she said, because she thought it would protect the baby from infections, which is not true. She thought that it was nutritionally better for the baby than formula — a difference that is not as clear-cut as she would like to think, nor as significant as her ample reading had led her to believe. I also guessed at another unstated reason in Arlene's mind: she saw nursing as a way for her to establish that the baby "needs me."

And there was a third prenatal interview that day. This one was different, not because Tom, the husband, came but because he did more talking than his wife, Margie, about breast-feeding. Like many people these days, Tom had combed the medical literature as well as the popular books. He knew the names of all the magic substances in breast milk, including lysozyme and lactoferrin, but he did not understand that infants who were lactose intolerant could not take breast milk or cow's milk. Nor did he know of the studies done on North American populations that had not been able to show any significant differences in the first-year infection rate between breast-fed and bottle-fed infants.

Tom had done a lot of work, but I couldn't help wondering why he was so interested in breast-feeding. Actually, Tom and Margie shared two concerns with many other couples. Their first concern was for what would be best for their child, and everyone seemed to say that nursing was the only choice. Margie and he had both read that bottle-feeding would make the child give up nursing — but Tom also knew that feeding was the baby's only predictable social time. So he understandably felt excluded. The second issue was sexual. Tom had read about how nursing women had orgasms, but he also had read that most doctors discourage intercourse for at least six weeks after delivery. Their sexual relationship was important to both of them, and frankly, Tom was jealous. As long as he could convince himself that breast-feeding was so good for the baby that there was no choice, then he was willing to accept it. Fortunately, we discussed a better compromise that he and Margie were happy with.

My answer to Nancy, Arlene, Margie and Tom, and all the rest is essentially the same. Nurse if you want to, don't if you don't. Among the hundreds of mothers in my practice, the vast majority nurse at least some of the time, and most are glad to have done so. But to be really satisfied with their decision, they have to have come to terms with what nursing really means to them. Before they begin, many women anticipate that nursing will be a spiritual high, a type of nirvana. But the typical experience is not the kind of transcendental state of mind or body that some expect it to be, and sometimes it is quite the opposite. Many women have periods during nursing when they feel angry over some of their unmet expectations, and yes, over the pain and discomfort that can accompany nursing. All the intellectual and emotional arguments favoring breast-feeding do not mean much when nipples crack or bleed, or when a duct becomes blocked and infected.

Part of the problem with breast-feeding traces back once again to the issue of control. Most mothers believe at the outset that all they have to do to make their baby nurse enthusiastically is to just do everything according to the instruction manuals. But this just isn't so. Much as you cannot control labor, you cannot make a child eat, not even a week-old infant. Like everything else in the relationship, nursing takes the cooperation of two people. True, you do have to learn certain techniques, but more important, you and your child have to discover each other's quirks and accommodate them to make nursing go smoothly. Some infants do not like body contact. Some do not like to be swaddled. Some lose their sucking rhythm if you interact with them while you feed them. For these reasons, and a dozen more, the picture-book portrait of the baby lying across his mother's chest, sucking avidly, and gazing fondly at her, and she at him, rarely happens in the first few days or weeks. When mothers who have allowed themselves to be seduced by such propaganda discover that their child refuses to behave that way, they can feel rejected. They tend to blame themselves for doing something wrong. Or they blame their milk, imagining there is something wrong with its taste or flow, or they blame their anatomy — breasts too small, too big, or whatever. None of these is the issue. The real issue is the child's behavior and what makes the baby comfortable.

Oftentimes all that is needed is for the mother to observe her child's reactions to nursing to see where the problem lies and make the necessary changes. For instance, you may find that if you stop talking to your daughter during the feeding she will do better. Do not force her to eat when she resists. Realize that your child is just as interested in her survival as you are, so she will feed when she needs to. If you worry that the baby is not competent to take care of such elementary things as getting enough to eat, then you will find it impossible to see how she can accomplish much more sophisticated activities, such as learning to self-calm. Further, you and your baby need to be comfortable with each other before you can build an attachment, and if her early encounters with you are associated with power moves, like your waking her every three hours to nurse when she prefers to sleep, she will have a harder time building a trusting relationship.

Another problem I find with nursing is that some women, when they discover that they do not enjoy breast-feeding, persist nonetheless, with increasingly negative feelings about themselves and the child. I can't think of a worse way to start a relationship. The baby may nurse, but since the social aspects of feeding are more important to the child than what he is fed, I'm sure he'd prefer to avoid all the negative feelings his mother has, which undoubtedly affect her behavior. Any baby caught in this situation would, I'm sure, vote to be fed formula if he were given the chance.

And let's not overlook the issue of exclusion that goes along with breast-feeding. In the first weeks of a baby's life, feeding is often the only time that the baby is awake. That puts the father of a breast-fed child in the situation of having little or no time to interact pleasurably with his child. Changing diapers is scarcely a satisfactory substitute for the social interaction that takes place around feeding. Consequently the father-child relationship has little chance to grow.

This feeling of exclusion on the part of fathers is heightened by the sexual overtones of breast-feeding for some mothers. Denied intercourse for weeks after delivery, and too exhausted for any other sexual activity with their spouse for some time after the baby's birth, some women discover in nursing an orgasmic outlet for their otherwise unexpressed physical drives. No wonder fathers tend to overreact against nursing when the baby is fussing or doesn't gain weight fast enough. They are understandably jealous of their wives' sexual release, physical relationship with the child, and exclusive social time with the baby, especially when the baby seems to be crying incessantly and not sleeping longer than two hours at night because the breast-feeding isn't going well. Then anger often erupts, in part as a result of this jealousy. If, instead of feeling totally excluded, the father can be involved at an early stage, as in a once- or twice-a-day bottle-feeding, then he is far more likely to work with the mother than against her.

So how do you resolve all the negatives and positives surrounding breast-feeding? The answer may not be immediately apparent to you. You certainly need to talk about it with your spouse well in advance of delivery, but you also need to be ready to change your mind later, without recriminations, if your first choice does not turn out to satisfy each of you as thoroughly as you had anticipated. That is what happened with Tom and Margie, with Nancy, and with Arlene, too.

It took some time to discover why Tom had such an exaggerated interest in breast-feeding. "Exclusion" is a serious question. So is a couple's sexual relationship. Tom was enchanted with feeding Lisa once or twice a day. He had an unexpected positive role, and Lisa didn't stop nursing after they started bottle-feeding on day five. Margie was not so exhausted since she was able to take a nap when Tom fed Lisa. She later said that she may have had one orgasm with nursing, but the whole pregnancy experience made her feel more sexual with Tom. Talking about it allowed them to start expressing the positive feelings each one should have been sharing all along. Like many couples, they had never talked openly about sex and what it meant to each one of them. Needless to say, their sexual relationship was not as bleak as either had imagined.

Once Nancy was convinced that she could nurse and go back to work, she chose to breast-feed. She found that with good nutrition, adequate sleep, and a positive attitude, a new mother's body is amazingly resilient in what it can do. Thus, she was able to nurse as the baby required in the first weeks while she was still at home full-time, and to express enough milk when she resumed work so that the baby could continue to have her milk, by bottle, for a long time after. When Nancy and her baby finally came to the stage when he was ready to be weaned, she could honestly say to herself that breast-feeding had been a pleasurable and satisfying experience for everyone.

For Arlene, however, the course was considerably different. The romantic fantasies surrounding nursing had been central to her desire to breast-feed, and she expected that, in nursing, Jason's comfort and health would be assured. Consequently, she nursed him every time he cried, at a cost to her own comfort and health. By two months she had had two bouts of mastitis, a painful breast infection, and was physically and emotionally exhausted. This wasn't the experience that she had anticipated. To make matters worse, when Jason was about thirteen weeks old, he refused to nurse for an entire day.

His father, frustrated by the continuous sound of his son's crying and convinced that, whatever else was going on, he must still be hungry, had gone out to the pharmacy and brought home baby formula. Jason quieted down instantly upon being presented with the bottle, and drained it quickly, confirming his father's diagnosis. But Arlene was hysterical. She called me that night, feeling rejected and upset, and hoping that I could give her some way to stir up her child's enthusiasm for nursing again. "I don't know why he isn't more attached to my breasts," she said, her voice cracking with emotion. "For the last three days all he does is look around when I try to nurse him. I can't believe this."

I told her that Jason was trying to give her a message. It wasn't that he didn't care about her, but he wasn't as enthusiastic about nursing as she was. He wanted to use it to feed, and she wanted to use nursing for her own social and emotional fulfillment. We talked about the ways that she could get more social time with Jason, but to make nursing simply feeding time. Reluctantly Arlene agreed to try to socialize and play *after* Jason fed, not during the nursing. She also found that he played longer and was more responsive if she didn't hold him so close and put him in his chair when he was through feeding.

Once Jason's mother compromised, he weaned her over about four weeks. He would suck for a few minutes until he had had enough to eat then defiantly stop. He never squirmed or cried unless Arlene tried to force him to nurse, which she did occasionally when she slipped back into old habits and expectations. But even long after Jason was happily taking all his milk from a bottle, Arlene continued to worry, to feel guilty, to blame his colds on the fact that she wasn't nursing him. She never really got over thinking that he needed nursing, when in reality she was the one with the real need.

Early abandonment of nursing happens fairly often, but usually it is the mother who revolts. Most babies find nursing an effective way to calm, and, so long as the mother goes along with it, they will continue to take advantage of the offering. Babies have been known to nurse continuously for hours or as frequently as twenty times a day, finding relief from whatever ails them in as little as one minute of sucking each time. Any mother caught in such an arrangement is going to have a hard time maintaining any self-image other than that of baby-sitter, because she virtually has no freedom to go anywhere or do anything that does not accommodate that relentless demand. Arlene was certainly headed for that kind of servitude, trying to use nursing for much more than feeding. Thankfully, Jason had called a halt first. He didn't like all the close socializing; he didn't even enjoy the body contact that much. He could not know it, but he saved himself a lot of pain later. Had nursing been allowed to become more than a feeding mechanism, had it become a way to calm to the exclusion of any other means, then weaning would have become an extended nightmare. What Arlene had intended to provide — support and security for Jason — would have become instead a dependency trap, and when eventually it was taken away for whatever reason, he would be left feeling deserted, helpless. Luckily for Jason and Arlene, that destructive pattern was never set in place.

Pregnancy, natural childbirth, bonding, and breastfeeding — all of these experiences have mythic components that many people, especially those who are approaching parenthood for the first, wondrously exciting time, find captivating. I can only restate my conviction that all of these experiences are more complicated than you may have been led to expect. False expectations have a disastrous aftereffect. For everyone's continued comfort and happiness, you will do well to approach these first aspects of parenting in a spirit of open-mindedness, ready to adjust, change, or totally reject the "rules" as you see fit.

Building a good relationship with your child requires giving up romantic dreams. As a parent you must make decisions based on what you know about yourself and your child, not what you wish were true. Not only must you be competent, but your child must be encouraged to be competent as well in her own way. Neither one of you has total control, only influence. In the next chapter I will talk about decisions — the ones you make and those that your child makes, yes, even as a newborn. These decisions quickly set a pattern of behavior. And it is the interlinking of your decisions that determines not only what she will do to self-calm, but how quickly she will master this indispensable skill system.

CHAPTER 3

Home from the Hospital

Why are many mothers more frightened of going home with a new baby than they are of labor and delivery? Why is this such an intimidating experience for both parents?

The reason is the decisions that have to be made. If parents do not give up the fantasies about childbirth or nursing or bonding that "guarantee" a perfect relationship, if they continue to rely on "maternal instinct" rather than learning from their decisions and willingness to set priorities, then coming home from the hospital can be a bad dream, which becomes a nightmare as each inadequate decision compounds the negative effects of the preceding ones.

Before the delivery, parents anticipate that going home from the hospital will be a relief, but that is rarely true. Much of the elation you felt in having given birth suddenly vaporizes when it's time to pack up and the nurse hands you your baby. No amount of reading, or bonding, or magical effects of natural childbirth ever prepares anyone for this moment.

The infant who was calm and wonderful in the hospital starts crying frantically — and may not stop for days. Parents who had planned to work as a team quickly become exhausted, angry, and divided; they blame each other for the problems that suddenly beset them. Relatives and in-laws swarm all over the house, full of "helpful suggestions" that sound suspiciously like criticisms. The telephone rings constantly with greetings and questions and more advice from well-wishing friends. While first-time mothers may be anxious to leave the hospital, it is little wonder that second- and third-time parents fantasize about staying two or three weeks, if only someone would let them.

And why should anyone expect it to be any different? Parenting is a new role, uncertain and undefined. You must put new decisions into action that immediately shape your relationship with your child. Your baby is a stranger who does not speak your language. You feel anxious, self-conscious, terribly vulnerable to mistakes. But these feelings, distressing as they may be, serve a noble purpose: they are part of what motivates you to work so hard and to put in so many hours with so little positive feedback from the baby.

Nothing will make the initial anxiety go away. This discussion, however, will give you ways to feel more sure of yourselves as parents just as quickly as possible. It will give you practical ways to make progress on your own terms, rather than waiting for your baby to change. And it will show you how your baby's behaviors, regardless of how irrational they seem, can help all of you adjust. The sooner you get the feeling that "I've got it right," the sooner you can begin to enjoy things as they are.

Defining a New Role

Parents often make coming home with the baby even more difficult than it has to be because they set unobtainable goals for themselves. Mothers, especially, are often burdened with the expectation that they should immediately know what to do with the baby, and when. Maternal instinct is supposed to give them instant wisdom. Unfortunately, fathers, in-laws, and grandparents frequently reinforce this idea. But instinct is not the answer. This business of being a parent is a learning experience that can only be done on the job. And if you feel confused about what to do next, how to play your new role, you can at least comfort yourself in the knowledge that your baby is feeling even more confused and more uneasy than you are.

Why so? After all, the nurses said she was such an easy baby. The answer is obvious when you think about it. When your child was in the hospital, she probably slept most of the time because she was still recovering from the delivery. Now that she is home, she feels overwhelmed, unfamiliar with the world and with herself as an independent being. To your consternation and despair, what seems to make her satisfied at 10 A.M. may not work at 4 P.M., even though the situation looks exactly the same and the cry sounds the same. It's not your fault. There is no right or wrong way at this point. At four days of age, she often does not have the experience to know what makes her feel best in a certain situation, and perhaps this isn't an identical situation from her perspective. Parental patience is much more valuable than any type of instinct.

There is another reason, however, that parents often feel so anxious and unsure. New parents tend to form lasting impressions of themselves and their child in the first few weeks of the baby's life. Minor transgressions and small failures seem to take on inordinate significance, as though such episodes, having happened once, are destined to repeat themselves forever. A parent who panics in the early stages may doubt himself or his partner for months and years to come. A baby who is difficult at first may have a hard time shaking that label later, even when he learns to self-calm and turns more agreeable. Life will be much less pressured the sooner you accept the liberating notion that what you see in the beginning is not necessarily part of a pattern. The reality is that there is no pattern right away, no set of "right answers" that you can hold on to from the start. Once you make up your mind that you expect to grow and change along with your developing baby, you will stand a very good chance of avoiding recurring problems and increasing tensions.

Daring to Experiment

No parent is perfect. In the first few weeks everyone makes countless wrong judgments or has moments when the baby is frantically crying and nothing seems to work. But there are ways to start getting the best of the situation. It takes work and time and resilience, but both fathers and mothers can learn.

The first and perhaps hardest decision is to dare to experiment. When everything about your daily life is in a state of flux, experimentation may sound like a dangerous solution, guaranteed to increase anxiety. On the other hand, since your baby is not preprogrammed, this is the only way you can find out what she responds to negatively and positively. If you hold her a certain way and she consistently cries more, then you can reasonably conclude that she does not feel comfortable being held that way, no matter what your best friend's experience is or what you read in your favorite baby book.

Try other ways, and when you find that she calms down consistently when a certain position is repeated, you can be fairly sure you are on the right track. Your willingness to try different things will also open new avenues to your daughter. For instance, it might take her many weeks to discover that sucking works as a wonderful calming mechanism, were you not to offer her your finger a few times. By experimenting, by offering different options, you'll more quickly feel that you are making progress on your own terms and not just waiting for your baby to change.

Success in this new adventure also requires parents to think for themselves. Every time you accept unquestioningly some universal statement about babies, you can bet that that "rule" will eventually get you or your child into trouble. Accepting such a rule prevents you from trying a new experimental response. For instance, when a new baby cries, someone will tell you that the reason is either that the baby has gas or that he is hungry. But this is, in fact, the right explanation only *some* of the time, and if you persist in applying only those solutions that deal with gas and hunger you will be wrong more often than you are right.

You have to believe that your baby can accurately communicate with you from the start if given half a chance, otherwise there is little hope of forming a relationship. If your good sense tells you that your crying baby can't be hungry right now, and if a reasonable amount of effort does not bring up a burp, then I urge you to forget what everyone has told you. Take a chance on some other possibilities, such as turning off the lights or talking softly to him, and see if one of these solutions isn't what your newborn really wants.

Getting it right involves trying to find as many ways as possible to help your baby. And it requires being willing to make your own judgments, even though Grandmother may adamantly tell you that you are wrong. And even if you are, so what? It will not be the last time, and no long-term damage has been done. Part of succeeding is making sure that small mistakes do not become set patterns of failure.

Helping Yourself

Since learning about the baby is your main priority right now, and that takes considerable time and energy, you will probably have to curtail some other activities that might seem like part of normal life but which end up being excesses in this very "un-normal" time.

Leaving the hospital requires little material preparation: some diapers, a couple of sets of baby clothes, a car seat if you drive, and bottles and formula if you are not going to nurse the baby. Yet I have seen fathers run themselves ragged shopping at the last minute for hundreds of items while their wives fret over making sure they have powders, toys, lotions, creams, and other items that they will never use. Your baby probably doesn't care if he sleeps in a cardboard box, and he certainly doesn't care whether he has on the latest designer outfit. You may think that you care, or that other people will think you are a bad parent if you do not have all of these things, but none of them is important. All that really matters right now is that you pay attention to your baby's well-being, and your own. You will be in a far better position to do so if you are not totally exhausted or worried silly about your credit-card balance.

Similarly, why be so concerned about how proficient you are at things like diapering and burping your baby? As the old saying goes, practice makes perfect, and by the end of the second week, these tasks will be second nature to you, something you can perform with your eyes closed. Changing diapers well may be a boost for your self-esteem, an early "success," but worrying about such chores only consumes your limited time and energy. You have enough else on your mind. And fear not, your baby is in no position to judge you on technique, at least not yet.

Finally, here are some practical, short-term things you can do for yourself to make the first days and weeks easier and more pleasant:

Unplug the Telephone

The telephone is, more often than not, an intrusion on a new family. It increases the sense of chaos. Most people who call end up making you feel that you are somehow stupid, foolish, incompetent, or that your baby is in some mysterious way odd, unresponsive, underweight, overweight, or subject to other nameless shortcomings. You begin to think that no other parent in history has ever made quite the botched mess that you are making. Somehow the calls always come just at the crucial moment when you have at last gotten your baby quieted, when she is finally nursing, when you have just fallen off to sleep, when your ten-day-old has just smiled for the very first time. The simplest way to avoid all this trouble is to rid yourself selectively of the intruder. Chances are your phone has one of those simple wall plugs, so it's an easy matter to unplug it; if not, turn off the bell volume control on the bottom of the set and put a pillow over the phone for good measure. (Let anyone who is likely to be concerned if you don't answer know that this is to be your habit for a while, lest they come rushing to the house to check up on you.) You can always plug the phone in again when you want to talk to a supportive friend or you need the advice of your pediatrician, but you will enjoy the feeling of being the one in charge.

Limit the Visitors

Rivaling the telephone as a nuisance and a hindrance are visitors. Do not give out open invitations to come see the baby unless you are ready to put up with a very unhappy infant and many sleepless nights. You have too much to do to spend a lot of time with social acquaintances in these first, harried days. Next week, or, preferably, next month, will be soon enough for baby to make his debut, so have people come to see him at your convenience, not theirs. If you feel that you must have someone over, then do it in the morning. Having visitors come in the afternoon tires you out more and makes the baby much fussier, for the same reason. Make your hospitality personal, but skip all the fancy preparations. No big spread of food, no grand efforts to dress up baby, both of which put enormous strain on the two of you. For the same reason, if the baby is asleep, never wake him up, even if Grandma thinks she will die unless she gets to rock him. If he is up but starts to fuss only five minutes into a visit, terminate his part of the visit without apologies.

Your baby's comfort comes before your visitor's at this point, and he's telling you he is uncomfortable. Remember that you set the rules. It is very easy to get trapped in a feeling of social obligation, and you may want to play the proud parent and show off your new son. But if he gets fatigued or overstimulated, then you, not the visitors, are going to pay the price that night and the next day. The question is, what are your priorities?

Get Others to Help

No matter how much you prepare, having a baby is tiring, and for most people fatigue is the biggest danger in the first few weeks. So if you can get help, take it, whether from understanding friends or family or someone hired expressly for the purpose. Use them wisely, not as nursemaids to the child but as housekeeping aides. Let them do household chores that you can't do right now. They can clean, they can cook, they can take your share of the car pool runs. That frees you to do your most urgent and important job, which is to learn about your baby, the sooner the better. Turning her care over to someone else for the first few days, by contrast, means that you risk missing so much. Things change in a hurry with a newborn, and starting your relationship ten days or two weeks later just puts you in a catch-up position. (I make an exception, of course, for any mother who is totally exhausted from a difficult delivery. It may be all she can do to care for herself. A nurse or a live-in relative who can be relied upon to be genuinely helpful to all concerned is then the best solution until the mother is strong enough to take over.)

Parent-to-Parent

My patients have some helpful firsthand observations to make about the first days at home with a new baby.

"Maybe part of the way you cope is that you don't admit how scared you really are. All kinds of thoughts and fears flood in about whether you really can be a mother. Something tells you that you will be able to learn to change diapers or dress the kid, so you concentrate on that, looking for some feeling of success. Obviously the baby needs to be taken care of, and you feel better about yourself when you do get those things right. But it really is misleading. What you are trying for is a relationship. That takes longer, and it is harder. I feel sorry for my friends who have settled for less in their relationships. They missed so much because they were so locked into taking perfect care of the baby that they never learned how to really care about the baby. If you don't see all the personality and understand all of the different things that you are doing, besides feeding them and clothing them, then it is really hard to fall in love with your baby. You are more of a servant than a parent. And a very tired one at that."

"I was such a fanatic about keeping Jill clean that I gave her a bath every day, sometimes twice a day, even though she hated it. It was only after our visit with you that I realized the bathing was the reason for her going berserk every night. I was breast-feeding, so I could clean her up with water. She didn't need a bath, and the nights got a whole lot better. It takes some time to realize the difference between what you have to do and what you think you have to do."

The Baby's Transition Behavior

However you handle your own coming home, the change from the hospital to "civilian life" is a major transition for the baby. It may not be as big a transition as being born, but then again, some babies act as though it were. For these children, the second change following so close on the first may be more than they can handle.

Consider it from the baby's perspective. He doesn't know what the unfamiliar motion of a car ride is all about, but he does know that something very disturbing is happening. His skin tells him that the benign temperature of his hospital environment has suddenly changed to the colder or warmer air of the outdoors. His nose informs him that the smells that he experienced in the hospital nursery or his mother's room have been replaced by countless other competing smells, all unfamiliar, some of them unpleasant. New noises, new lights, sounds, and textures — constant, unexpected changes must be encountered. He is not familiar with anyone, including his parents, and, often as not, endless strangers are poking and pressing him. Altogether, the baby's experience of going home from the hospital is not very different from what yours would be if I took you blind-folded and deposited you without explanation in Outer Mongolia. You would live through it, but you wouldn't enjoy it. In sum, Going Home Day is Chaos Day for the baby.

As a result, some babies cope with transition by fussing constantly; others sleep almost uninterruptedly through the period, which can last as long as five days. Don't expect to be able to predict which way your child will behave on the basis of how she behaved in the uterus, or even in the hospital. Just accept the fact that she is doing her best, in her own way, to feel more safe and less assaulted by sensations she does not understand. You can help your child by recognizing her needs and by doing your best to make this transition period more comfortable for all of you.

The larger share of infants — about 80 percent — fall

into the category of fussers. Fussers have a rough time adjusting, and they want everyone to know it. They seem to be protesting. Some of the fussers start to get out of control even before you leave the hospital. Others manage to wait until everyone is in the car; that, at least, saves the embarrassment of having the nurses watch you floundering. Still other fussers wait until you get them home before starting their floor show.

The typical pattern of behavior goes something like this: as you ride down in the elevator, your baby in your arms, he feels alternately stiff and squirmy. As you leave the hospital, the cold January air makes him grimace, and then he starts to cry during the clumsy process of putting him in the car seat for the first time. Having just been nursed an hour ago, it seems unlikely that he needs to be fed. Besides, it's only a twenty-minute ride, so you decide to go ahead with putting him into the car seat, fussing notwithstanding. Five minutes later, the baby is screaming. Pulling off the road, you find that he does not need to be changed, and when you try to nurse him, he sucks briefly, seeming to settle down, but starts to fuss as soon as you move to put him back in his seat. Or he starts to nurse and then spits up. After twenty minutes of trying to get him quieted, you decide to make a mad dash for home. Perhaps the motion of the car finally gets him to settle down for a few minutes.

Before you get through the front door, the fussing and wailing start all over again. His diaper is wet, but changing him doesn't change the behavior. You pace back and forth with him in your arms for twenty minutes, while he cries the whole time. Then, unaccountably, he falls asleep. You're not sure what turned the trick — was it the walking, or did he just wear out from his own exertions?

Regardless, he is back up fifteen minutes later, howling this time. You try to nurse him. He works at it fitfully for three minutes, and then dozes off again until you try to put him down. He rouses, fussing, and then spits up the feeding all over you. You change him, and he goes back to sleep for half an hour. After another fitful three-minute nursing, he goes down for fifteen minutes. Back up again, you quiet him this time by rubbing his back. For about forty minutes. Then he is up again, crying, just as Grandmother calls. (You haven't gotten around to unplugging the phone yet.) Wearily, you hand Junior over to his father, while you fend off queries about whether you shouldn't be giving him formula, or cereal, instead.

At this point you want a drink, and you are angry at the baby's father, who, understandably, is having his second. The phone call has made you more anxious, and now when you take the baby back to put him in his bassinet he starts to scream right away. You hand him back and, wonder of wonders, he goes to sleep for about an hour in Dad's lap. Meanwhile, you rub your breasts with some cream because they are getting pretty sore after being chewed on almost constantly for the past four hours. Just as you begin to relax, the baby starts to cry again. Like the previous feedings, this one is short, and he drops off in a fitful sleep. You begin to wonder about Grandma's advice, and decide that you can do without any more calls today. To protect yourself, you unplug the phone.

Days like this with your newborn are hellish to live through, and unfortunately, they can go on for five days nonstop. You frequently wonder whether any of you are going to make it through alive. Adoption looks like it might have been a better alternative. A thirty-minute walk outside while Dad struggles with the baby is worth more than you can say.

Why is this happening? Am I doing something wrong? you wonder. No, it's not your fault. Going home is just too much of a change for your baby to handle all at once. The more you try to calm the baby down, the more stimulated she gets, and often that just makes her cry louder and longer. All this crying, of course, causes her to swallow excess air, so she gets gas, which complicates things more. And to complete the vicious cycle, as you get more frantic, your baby mirrors your feelings in her behavior, with tensions mounting ever upward.

Such fussy, erratic, transition behavior is especially hard on nursing mothers. Everyone swears that the baby is starving. This is rarely true. The baby who feeds for two minutes and then goes to sleep is not looking for food but for comfort, especially a way to go to sleep. If he wants to eat, he'll eat. Meanwhile, by the third day, with your nipples bleeding, and people still saying he's starving — even though he urinates eight times a day and has a bowel movement after each feeding — you are having a hard time keeping your perspective on just how "blessed" an event this business of motherhood is anyway. About the only thing you feel confident about is your ability to change diapers — you have become a master at it, maybe sooner than you would have wished!

No techniques can completely eliminate this kind of nightmare for the majority of babies who experience going home as unpleasant and disorienting. But I tell parents they can shorten the nightmare by cutting down on all the transitions the baby is exposed to. The less stimulation the better. That means no visitors. The baby needs to be in a dark, quiet environment, and she needs to be handled as little as possible. Feedings should be all business. I recommend socializing only after the feeding, not during it. And make the exchanges very short, or else your attempts to play will likely end abruptly in crying. The more sensitive and reactive the baby, the more careful the parents need to be. If you make your newborn's world comfortable, chances are he will adjust to his new life in a few days, after which you can gradually relax a little. If you try to force him to get used to the world, relaxation will be a long way off.

If 80 percent of babies fall into the hard-times-ahead category, the other 20 percent take a different approach to going home. They tend to shut down as a way of screening out stimulation. They ride home without much fuss, feed well, and go to sleep quickly when they are put down in the early afternoon. And then they don't wake up again until ten or eleven o'clock at night. The baby looks very alert, feeds well, stays awake for a while, and then goes back to sleep for another eight to twelve hours. This may sound ideal, but, ironically, it can be just as unnerving to parents as the baby who fusses constantly. After two or three days of this, they are likely to wonder if their child is sick, given his lack of activity.

I tell parents that if the child is alert and responsive when awake, and if she feeds well the few times that she is up, then the baby is fine. If you're worried, check her temperature, or if you see any other signs that you don't understand, call your pediatrician.

The peace and tranquility that this kind of transition behavior allows is not unshakable, however. It can be shattered if the parents decide to wake the baby when he does not want to be awakened, for example, to feed him. Some well-meaning friend will have convinced the parents that their baby will get sick if they let him go eight or nine hours without food. Wanting to show the baby off to a visitor is another temptation to wake him. Whatever the reason, when sleep is interrupted parents are in for a terrible surprise. The baby starts to cry. But unlike the Fusser, who will eventually calm down, the Sleeper loses control totally when his transition behavior is interfered with. The crying goes on for hours, regardless of what the parents do. Dealing with a Sleeper under these conditions can be one of the worst experiences that anyone can have with an infant.

If you are lucky enough to have a baby who reacts to transition by trying to sleep through it, leave well enough alone. Don't wake her up because you think she needs to eat or needs to socialize. She has no interest in starving herself, and she won't. Just like the Fusser, she will settle down to more normal behavior when she feels comfortable in her new environment.

A Comfortable Environment

The main elements of a more comfortable environment for a newborn are light, sound, and activity level. Discovering the combination that can make your child feel more at "home" can only be done through experimentation. Each baby will respond in a way uniquely his.

The logical place to begin is with sleep. Sleep is the critical support system for the parents and the child. The parents have two goals: they need the infant to sleep for a long block of time, rather than in short bursts, and they need that block to be at night, during the hours when everyone else normally sleeps.

The key to getting a long block of time is never to wake the child when she is sleeping. This only disorganizes an infant, so that the rest of her sleep that night (and perhaps for many nights to come) is more erratic. In the beginning, of course, she is likely to wake up every two to four hours during the night without your help. Her body is entering a period of very fast growth, and because she can take in nourishment at the rate of only two to three ounces per feeding, she gets genuinely hungry rather often. So be prepared for your baby to fall asleep at the "wrong time" and be awake at the "wrong time." Don't try at this stage to interfere. Better to take a nap yourself. Eventually, the baby will move her "time zone" to one more accommodating to the family's habits, but in the meantime you need your sleep, too, even if it's not exactly at a time you would prefer it.

Sleeping at night doesn't just happen for infants, it has to be taught. The learning process works through subtle persuasion, which should begin immediately. Your baby needs to learn that darkness is the time to sleep, and daylight the time to be awake. There are many factors that go into persuading your child to set his body clock to such a schedule, but the primary one is social time. Since socializing is his highest priority, the baby will organize his alert time around the best social response that he can get. Conversely, his sleep time will eventually settle around times when social response is least rewarding or even nonexistent.

So, from the start, you want your responses to make nighttime boring. Conversely, you want to make your daytime together maximally attractive.

Making the night boring is not very hard. When parents get up to answer a cry, they need to keep the baby's room dark, and they should attend to the task at hand rather than playing, talking, or making prolonged eye contact with the infant. If the parent can doze off during the feeding, that is fine, too. I wouldn't change the baby unless she is a mess, and I wouldn't do anything else that extends your interaction in any way, unless it is absolutely essential to your baby's comfort, health, or safety. Of course, the baby may have other ideas. If your newborn is like the majority, she wants dark and quiet and thrives on your undistracted attention. She probably thinks that two in the morning is a grand time to be up and to play. You may be tempted to go along, at least at first, because it's the best social time you get with her all day. But resist. Your long-term goal is to have the baby bright and alert in the daytime, and now is the opportunity to set that pattern in place, even if you cannot hope to reap the benefits immediately.

In order to encourage the baby to stay awake when you are, you also want to give some consideration to what sort of daytime milieu you are offering. Is it attractive to him? To find out, watch how the baby responds when you make various adjustments to his environment. Observe his facial expression, his breathing rate, his skin color and his body tone, and the motion of his arms and legs. He is comfortable when he smiles, has a smooth respiratory rhythm, pink skin, normal body tone, and smooth movements of his limbs. He's not comfortable when he frowns, cries, has erratic breathing with mottled skin and blue hands or feet, and his body tone is limp or very stiff with awkward motions of his arms and legs (see Chapter 4, Communication, for more detail).

Typically, your child's behavior will give you the answers to how much stimulation she can handle comfortably. Very possibly, she will favor a room that is a little darker and quieter than you ordinarily keep it, at least in the beginning. If the television or radio are turned on, be sure they are on low volume, and preferably not in the same room with the baby. You may love Berlioz, but she may not. If you open the shade and she grimaces or cries, then that is probably just too much light. The colored mobile may have to be taken down and the bright balloon wallpaper covered with a sheet for a few weeks if each time she sees them you get a negative response.

Habituation: The Unknown Skill

Creating a daytime environment that is attractive to the
infant makes it less likely that he will fuss or try to
shut down. Fussing obviously takes energy, but so does
"playing possum," as I call it. When things are too much
for your baby he may not cry or fuss. He may look as
though he is asleep, but he's not. We have all seen
babies sleep through big gatherings — and then heard
tales about how they cry all night or the next day. That
is because playing possum, or shutting down, or "habituating," to use the technical term, costs energy. It's
tiring.

Put in layman's terms, habituation is the ability to
"tune out," and it is truly one of the most amazing
skills a newborn possesses. The baby practicing it looks
as though she is sleeping, but habituation, unlike sleep,
does not replenish energy. Rather, it consumes energy. True, her heart rate decreases, and she has less
motor tone, just as in sleep. But there is little change,
none of the normal variation in respiratory rate, heart
rate, or body tone. Habituation is less stressful than
being fully awake but it is still draining. Unless parents
recognize this and decrease the stimulation load, the
infant becomes more and more fatigued.

One way to recognize the difference between sleeping and habituating is to observe the child's behavior
when he "wakes." The infant who is genuinely asleep
and wakes spontaneously is responsive, alert, and re-
freshed. The infant who is habituating wakes and is
quickly fussy and irritable. He acts exhausted rather
than rested. Forced to protect himself from too much

noise, light, activity, or handling, the habituating baby goes into his cocoon. He's hoping you'll get the message and put him someplace more comfortable.

Habituation is very valuable to you and your newborn, especially in the first few weeks when you are trying to learn about each other. It is, in fact, one of her most useful modes of communication at the time. When your five-week-old infant tunes out all day, when she appears to be sleeping all day, you can be pretty sure that she is sending a message that some activity, some stimulus, perhaps some combination of factors, is causing her to be overstimulated. Often you can recognize other cues before habituation begins. For instance, during a feeding, she loses her sucking rhythm. Or while you are holding and talking to her, her body tone becomes erratic; she shows a slight tremor, and despite all of your efforts she goes to "sleep" and never finishes the feeding. She awakens two hours later, fussy. You try to nurse her, but she quits even sooner this time. The baby is shutting down. She is telling you that she cannot handle what is going on around her: too much light, or noise, or perhaps too much sociability on your part during the feeding. When this sequence is repeated several times during the day, the baby eventually shuts down for longer and longer periods of time.

Habituation is actually a continuum of behavior. A baby can *shut down* when the level of stimulation gets to be too much. He closes his eyes, often bringing his arms or knees up toward his chest. As soon as the offending stimulus stops — for instance, the stereo is turned down, the lights are lowered, or Grandmother

pulls her face back from six to eighteen inches away —
the baby "wakes up," opens his eyes, and becomes
more alert. If repeatedly challenged, the periods of
"sleep" are longer and he will fuss rather than return
to alert, socially responsive behavior. In more extreme
circumstances, the baby will *shut off*. For example, there
is the one-month-old who, paradoxically, sleeps through
his christening party despite the attention of thirty
adults. The infant who shuts off will appear to go to
sleep for hours, regardless of the surroundings. He will
resist attempts to rouse him, and when he does awake
he cries and is inconsolable.

Habituation, if you misread it as sleep, has a terrible
cost. If this goes on for days, the result is that the baby
who was so "good" last week when she was sleeping all the time is now unbearable. The infant who
"sleeps" all day disintegrates into ceaseless "colic" from
four to ten every night. Or the baby who has "long
naps" wants to nurse every hour all evening. And then
she's up every two hours all night. Disorganized and
fussing, she nurses for two minutes and then goes back
to sleep for forty-five minutes or an hour, only to awake
shrieking. She nurses two minutes, fitfully, and repeats the process in another hour. She isn't hungry; if
she were she would feed and be satisfied. Exhausted
and miserable, she's using the nursing to try to feel
better, to put herself to sleep through sucking or other
calming effects of the feeding. The parents, no better
off, are sleepless and confused because they can't figure out why this child, who "slept for three hours"
that afternoon, is so grouchy and fatigued.

Like any other skill, some infants are better at habituation than others. And even children who are very good at it cannot always depend on habituation to avoid trouble. Occasionally, the infant waits too long before tuning out or the initial stimulus overload is too great, so that the infant does not have sufficient reserves of energy to retreat into habituation. Then he collapses into ceaseless fussing and becomes inconsolable. It should also be noted that habituation is a short-lived skill, lasting a matter of weeks or months at best. It may disappear overnight, but habituation is a newborn skill that generally wanes slowly after eight to twelve weeks.

So take heed of habituation and learn from it while it is there to teach you. Discover the warning signals that happen before habituation occurs, and learn what your baby perceives as overstimulation. The same things will probably still be bothering her weeks later, only then, instead of habituating, she will cry more often. By adjusting the environment to make it more comfortable, you have a good chance of preventing the tremendous drain on your baby's energy that habituation takes.

Fatigue

One of the keys to getting your child on a normal day-and-night schedule is to avoid fatigue. In the first weeks, both parents and infants are tired from lack of sleep and generally overextended, overwhelmed, and overstimulated. Regardless of age, fatigue makes all of us react less competently. Emotions get distorted. It is more difficult for you to observe and for your baby to learn. The combination can have disastrous effects on your relationship.

Be scrupulous in protecting yourself as well as your baby from fatigue. In the first rush of enthusiasm about the baby, parents frequently overextend themselves without realizing the cost. After two weeks at home, if you hear yourself saying with a slightly manic tone in your voice, "Things aren't too bad. We're up only three times a night," then you know you need some respite. Such a regimen is exhausting, and you cannot help but suffer physically and mentally from the strain. Every relationship in the family is bound to suffer as well.

Another indicator that you have crossed the safety margin of fatigue and are entering dangerous territory is when you begin to feel negative about everything, when you find yourself fighting with your spouse over small issues, or when you find yourself compromising long-held career decisions for lack of energy to think them through carefully.

Parent-to-Parent: Dealing with Exhaustion

"One of my fantasies during the pregnancy was that the time at home following delivery was going to be a kind of vacation from work. I was going to have lots of time to see all of my friends, something I really missed on the job. This was going to be my time to catch up. And I was going to show off the baby. Well, some days I should have canceled the visits. I was too tired, unless I had people come in the morning. And oftentimes I could not let them play with John because, although he liked the attention, he was often a wreck for the rest of the day. He didn't sleep and I didn't sleep. That only made the next day worse yet. He would fuss all the time, I would be punchy, and then I'd end up getting mad at him, or my friends, or my husband because I felt so drained."

"People always say that it is easier with your second child. It wasn't. I found it tiring just taking care of a twenty-month-old, let alone having a new baby. And since I hadn't been successful breast-feeding my first, I was nervous. Every time she peeped at night I would be up with her. I never got any rest in the day, and then I was awake every two hours at night. Many times I would go in and Sara was just fussing in her sleep. I knew that things were out of hand when my husband, Myron, said one morning that he was even willing to have my mother come for a week. I looked so awful that he was afraid that I was going to get sick."

"Every time she was the slightest bit wet I would change her. She was always immaculately dressed. Of course, I was still trying to do all the cooking and the cleaning. By the fifth or sixth day I felt sort of numb, and I fell asleep at seven o'clock. Luckily, Pete gave her a bottle, or I would have collapsed. But he couldn't be up all night either, and by the second week I just had to stop doing certain things. So the house wasn't as clean. No one else noticed but me."

"The feeling of being under constant demand was a major part of my fatigue. Eventually I learned that some things could wait. Just because Steven's diapers needed changing, I would not necessarily jump to take care of it. He rarely cried, fortunately, and if I felt like a nap at the moment, I would take it. That tiny act of independence was somehow very important to me."

"I can remember how compulsive I was with Jamie. I was pretty tired when we left the hospital. The nurses were always bringing her in saying that she had to be fed, but she never wanted to nurse. I didn't sleep any of those nights wondering what was wrong with me that she wouldn't nurse. At least being in a different environment at home eventually cured that, but I was still sleepless worrying that I had to be the perfect mother."

"Sometimes in the first weeks you make tough choices. You feel trapped in the house. You're too tired to get up in the morning, but going out in the afternoon just disrupts the baby too much. You long to talk to somebody on the phone when he sleeps, but you know that you really have to nap yourself. That makes you feel even more isolated."

"My labor lasted more than a day. I didn't bounce back. Even two weeks later I could tell that I still wasn't right. I simply couldn't do everything. I had to make choices. I had to use bottles, occasionally, because I was too drained out. Sometimes I took a bath and Joy, my daughter, did not. It helped me to feel better, and sometimes that psychological lift was as important as anything else."

New Discoveries

Eventually the transition period comes to a natural end. For most families it is a matter of one week, two at the most. Many parents now find themselves entering a kind of honeymoon period with their new baby. Their own emotional and physical energy has returned, which gives them an enormous boost, but more important, the baby has settled down to some kind of routine that the parents can recognize and accommodate to. The baby's ability to shut himself off or play possum also provides a protective cocoon for a period of a few weeks. With everyone feeling better and more competent, it is time to examine the structure of the new family and how each member is faring in the equation. The baby may seem easier to live with, but other changes are taking place. This is not necessarily a honeymoon for the parents.

It's not uncommon for the new father to feel displaced and resentful. That is in large part because he may not have figured out what role he is to play with the baby. Centuries of tradition taught us that men are superfluous in the nursery, and the new father probably had this pattern reinforced in the models his own parents displayed in raising him. Today, he is being told to get involved, but he has no ready role models to guide him. He feels awkward, unschooled, even foolish in others' eyes as he gropes about trying to make

himself useful. The new father may also feel jealous —
jealous of his wife, who has a better, closer relationship with the baby than he does, and jealous of the
baby, whose claim on his wife has in many ways sup-
planted his own.

If the mother is nursing, then the father is automatically shut out of the feeding routines, often the only
time the baby is awake and fully responsive in the first
days and weeks. This feeling of being second place, or
even no place, is not easy for anyone, but it is probably
harder for men raised in our society. And the role of
"mother's helper" — all that seems left to them — only
makes most men feel more humiliated. Despite the
stereotypes and the roadblocks, many new fathers attempt to make early connections with the baby, only
to have their efforts foiled by bad timing. Usually they
take the first week off — the transition period — on the
reasonable premise that the recuperating mother needs
their help most just then. And in a practical sense they
are right to be there. But if they also hope to get to
know the baby then, they are bound to be disappointed. As we have seen, the baby is totally engrossed in fussing or sleeping the first week and unlikely
to give any sort of positive feedback. Furthermore, the
first week is not when many of the important marriage
issues can be addressed. Finally, going back to work
fatigued and disappointed will affect job performance,
which undercuts future attempts to learn to be a father.

On the other hand, the "honeymoon period" is a
logical time for new parents to reassess career and personal decisions. Now that the baby is no longer some-

thing imagined but a real, living person, do the plans you made months ago still feel comfortable? How committed to parenthood are you? Does going back to work in six weeks still feel right to the mother? Does constant traveling on the job or staying late night after night make sense to the father? If someone in the family must compromise for the good of the family as a whole, are both partners agreed on who is to be the one? Does the decision stand on its own merits or is it based on traditional gender roles that may not really make sense in this situation?

Couples who have begun to discuss their options openly and honestly during pregnancy have a head start on coming to some kind of understanding with each other. But even with practice these are very hard questions to face, and your final answers may surprise you. They may discomfit your in-laws or your employer, too, and you will have to deal with their judgments. But the sooner you start resolving the questions, the better and more sensible your plans for the future will be.

Many men realize that their current job does not give them the time or the energy to be the always-available parent they had meant to be. More and more, many new mothers are also having to come to grips with these painful realities. One way to gain more time and energy for parenting is to change careers or to accept a job with less responsibility and less pay.

But understandably, most couples find it hard if not impossible to think about scaling down economic goals at the very time that the family is expanding. So what usually happens is that when more time must be found for the baby's sake, the only career change that is considered is the mother's — regardless of whose career prospects are better or who is actually most comfortable caring for the child.

No one can tell your family what division of responsibilities is going to make the most sense, financially and emotionally, for now and for the long run. But one look at the social revolution in our midst suggests that there are more good ways to run a family than anyone would have guessed a generation ago. Have you given them fair consideration or are you simply following your parents' orthodoxy? Most couples give lip service to being modern and enlightened, but how many really look at their career choices with a contemporary perspective? Certainly the assumption by men — or by women, for that matter — that the new mother should automatically put her own career goals aside, or take a less demanding job because she is the mother, is dangerous and out of step with reality. Child-rearing, as fulfilling as the experience is, is not a perfect substitute for the rewards of working, which have their own distinct incentives. Quite apart from the financial rewards, a career offers the individual self-esteem, intellectual stimulation, and the gratification of working with other adults who share the same interests and concerns. So be sure in negotiating the career decisions for the family that you take some time to find a comfortable balance for everyone.

If you have a very reactive and sensitive child, for example, who demonstrates early that she is going to take a long time learning to self-calm, then you can assume from the start that going back to work is likely to be a struggle for everyone. Instead of leaving the mother to cope on her own, more or less twenty-four hours a day, with all the frustrations and anger that is likely to produce, you and your spouse might consider splitting the early weeks between you, each one working part-time, if possible. You may assume that your employer would never agree to this, but you'll never know if you don't ask. Likely he or she has gone through the same adjustments with a child.

In some families, where the father is the calmer, less-anxious personality or where his job requirements are more flexible, it may actually work better for the mother to work full-time and the father part-time until the baby settles down. In almost every situation where there were two working parents before the birth, however, both individuals will need to maintain some career involvement following the transition weeks with the baby. Even if the big push to be vice president no longer seems so important, few men or women can give up the personal benefits of a job to stay home with a baby full-time. In some European countries, extended parental leave is possible, though I realize few employers or work situations in this country are ready to tolerate that sort of arrangement. Extended leave gives parents time to sort out their relationship, and to discover what activities really matter to them. By then, too, they know what to expect of the baby, physically and emotionally. They have a schedule they can live with, and their child can self-calm. (When your baby can self-calm it's easier to leave him with someone else. He's more self-sufficient and you don't feel as though he's suffering without you.) Everyone is functioning well enough at this point to enjoy one another, and, because they are

confident of the situation at home, parents' perfor-
mances on the job improve proportionately.

Parents Helping Each Other

Working with many new parents, I have developed the
following guidelines which have proven highly successful in helping dual-career parents get to know their
baby and maintain the emotional strength of their relationship while at the same time providing satisfactory career involvement for both father and mother.
Even if father or mother is going to stay home full-
time, most of these ideas will help maintain a health-
ier, happier marriage while making each of you a better parent.

Time with Your Spouse

Even if you have to hire a baby-sitter, try to set aside
at least two times a week when you and your spouse
can talk in a relaxed and freewheeling manner for a
couple of uninterrupted hours. You need to stay in touch
more than ever right now because many things that
are happening to you are new and need sorting out. It
is understood that you won't always see eye to eye on
everything but you need to get your feelings out.

Father's Role

Short of breast-feeding, there is little that fathers cannot learn to do in the way of child care. No one likes
changing diapers, so share the chore. Anyone can give

a bath, put on a fresh nightie, or put the baby to bed, so find ways to divide the tasks between you. The more fathers are involved with the little tasks of child-raising, especially feeding, the more often they will be the ones to witness the smiles, to see the new behaviors, to get the positive responses that make parenthood so rewarding. Helping each other now sets a valuable precedent for shared parenting later on. Remember, the patterns you set over the first two or three months tend to continue. As a team you will discover more than one parent could exploring alone.

Both parents need to have ways, as individuals, to relate with the infant. In the beginning, most social time revolves around feeding, and nursing mothers have a natural avenue for building a relationship during the many times a day they breast-feed. But what comparable exchange can the father have if the baby is nursing? I urge parents in my practice to arrange feedings so that Dad gives the baby one bottle a day, preferably in the morning, when the baby is most alert and Dad is rested. (The bottle time could be at night, but chances are no one will be at his best.) Even with the one-week-old, there is no need to worry that this will upset the baby's nursing routine. The mother can express the two or three ounces needed for this once-a-day feeding, or you can use formula. And the baby will continue to breast-feed just fine.

Morning Social Time

In the first few months, babies are more socially responsive in the morning. At 5 or 6 P.M. they are usually no fun to be with. Therefore, fathers generally get more out of their limited time with the infant if they leave for work later in the morning and come home later at night than may have been their custom before the baby's arrival. The same is true for mothers who have to go back to work soon after they deliver. An hour at 7 A.M. will be much more enjoyable than time in the early evening.

Parental Leave

If you are a working parent with limited vacation time or parental leave, you will do better to take time off from work when the child is seven to ten weeks of age, as opposed to the first two weeks. At this point you will be better able to learn about who your baby is and how he uses his social skills and his ability to self-calm. By this time, too, your baby will probably be closer to being on some kind of predictable schedule, so that more time is available for play, for you and your spouse to be with each other, and for taking care of other personal needs. By this point it should also be easier to see where your marriage stands and what career decisions have to be made.

Sharing

Both parents need to maintain some semblance of the adult relationships and responsibilities they had before the baby was born. Look at job responsibilities and commuting and travel time. What can you do to make the situation equitable? Work out between you who is going to be responsible for staying home when the baby is sick or when your child-care arrangements have to be adjusted — the care-giver is sick, the nursery is closed because of a holiday, that sort of thing. And watch out that you don't fall into one common trap that can cause smoldering resentments. Whether you have separate bank accounts or not, be sure you each contribute to child care costs equally. In families where the mother's paycheck is largely taken up with child-care bills and the father's check goes to cover the sometimes more glamorous expenses of family life, the mother can end up feeling either that the baby is, in effect, "her responsibility," or that her contribution to the family's main income is little, or both.

In seeking a balance, many parents end up taking turns so earnestly that they never see each other and never share any time together as a threesome. When one parent is home, the other works; and vice versa. While this sounds fair and reasonable, it never seems to work for very long. The family unit needs nurturing as much as individual relationships do. Make sure that you save some time for the three of you, even if the baby is only an observer of household chores. She won't get bored. She'll quickly manage to get involved, even if only chattering with you. And there is no reason why a grandmother or grandfather, or aunt or uncle, or even a baby-sitter can't watch your three-week-old while the two of you see an afternoon matinee or have brunch together one weekend day. Your marriage should not be put on hold when you have a baby. I have seen too many couples try this and end up with no marriage at all. That is not in anyone's best interest — especially not your child's.

Practical Suggestions

There are a few other medically related issues that frequently become unwarranted distractions for parents during the first weeks after childbirth. Without even knowing it, you have probably absorbed a certain amount of old wives' tales about what they mean and what you should do about them. As the list below indicates, these matters are generally very manageable, even by the most inexperienced parent.

Jaundice

Jaundice is a yellowing of the skin and eyes. It is caused by higher than normal accumulations of the pigment bilirubin, a byproduct of the breakdown in the liver of hemoglobin from red blood cells. In the mature liver the pigment is disposed of virtually as fast as it is generated, but in more than half of healthy newborns the liver is not yet able to keep up with the supply. Excess bilirubin circulates throughout the blood system, appearing as a yellow skin tone, accumulating from head to toe, peaking on or about the third day, when the bilirubin level in the blood is 8–12 mg%. Some babies go higher. Once considered a cause for alarm, no matter what its level, it is now generally treated only when it rises to the mid to high teens. The condition typically dissipates and disappears by the end of the first week. More persistent cases, however, require medical examination and, possibly, intervention.

There is also the phenomenon of so called "breast milk jaundice." The exact cause of this problem is unknown. What happens is that the nursing baby becomes increasingly jaundiced on the fourth, fifth, or sixth day of life. It has been attributed to a pregnanediol compound in the mother's milk by some, but not all, medical investigations. Don't despair. The cure is easy. Feeding the baby formula for 36–48 hours at your pediatrician's discretion causes a drop in the bilirubin, and then the mother can resume nursing.

Temperature

Normal body temperature for a baby tends to fluctuate more than an adult's. Though a rectal temperature of 98.6 degrees can still be designated normal, such factors as time of day, air temperature, clothing, food intake, and mild activity can temporarily elevate or decrease the reading by as much as a few tenths of a degree. If the baby is doing well and is appropriately dressed, then there is no reason to check the temperature. On the other hand, a temperature reading is a very useful, sometimes critical piece of information for gauging sickness and ought to be done whenever you suspect that the baby is struggling with some ailment, mild or serious.

The best way to take the temperature is with a rectal thermometer because it senses interior temperatures more accurately than measuring under the baby's arm or using a strip on the forehead. Simply coat the specially designed short round bulb of the rectal thermometer with a lubricant, such as petroleum jelly, and gently slide it into the rectum about an inch. Leave it in for a couple of minutes. The reading on the thermometer is the baby's real body temperature; an axillary temperature reading (taken under the arm) is typically lower and must be adjusted for accuracy. Rectal temperatures of less than 98 or greater than 99.5 warrant a call to your pediatrician.

Clothing

Someone will always be telling you that your baby is overdressed or underdressed. You can't do much about that, but to avoid uncertainty on your part, follow these simple guidelines, indoors and out. If the air temperature is greater than 80°F, the baby needs the same amount of clothing as you are wearing, for instance, a single cotton shirt on top. From 70 to 80°F, the baby needs one more layer than you have on, and if it is less than 70°F, the baby needs two more layers than you are wearing, plus a hat, for the simple reason that he has far less body mass in proportion to his surface area than you do and, consequently, loses body heat at a far faster rate.

Cord Care

It is important to take scrupulous care of your baby's umbilical cord stump to prevent infection from developing. Keep the stump and navel area clean and dry. Wipe them thoroughly (especially where the cord meets the abdominal wall) at every diaper change with rubbing alcohol or whatever your pediatrician recommends, and fold the diaper down in front in such a way as to keep the area dry and free from contact. Parents sometimes take shorcuts on cord care for fear the cleaning is painful to the baby, but there is little pain involved when done properly. Normally, the cord will come off naturally in about seven to ten days, at which time there will probably be minor bleeding over the course of one or two days. Should you detect unusual redness or heat around the navel, or foul-smelling discharge, call your pediatrician.

Rashes

Newborns may have a number of minor skin eruptions that are generally harmless and disappear without treatment. In the first few days many newborns have a rash that looks like pimples. Such a rash can be a sign of infection, but most often it is a normal occurrence called erythema toxicum, which disappears spontaneously. Another pimple-like rash generally occurs in the second to eighth week. It looks just like miniature acne, although there may be a dry crusting that accumulates. The distribution is generally over the face and neck. There are many ways to treat this, but the primary cause is that the skin is too oily. This rash often occurs in conjunction with "cradle cap" — a yellowish brown crusting on the scalp. It may look dry and scaly, but if you rub it you'll find that underneath the crusting it is oily. There are several different methods for treating the rash or the cradle cap, so ask your baby's physician for advice.

Birthmarks

Despite their popular name, patches of discolored skin or "birthmarks" are rarely present at birth, but appear, if at all, in the first few weeks. The majority are hemangiomas, concentrations of tiny blood vessels in the skin, which can appear as flat or raised patches of pink, red, or purple skin anywhere on the body. A second type is caused by a concentration of pigment, causing the skin in one or more places to become darker. Hemangiomas are almost always harmless, and though they may increase in size during the first year, they generally disappear later without leaving any scars or other marks. The significance of the second type of birthmark is currently a matter of medical debate and should be discussed with your baby's physician.

Visiting and Guests

Assuming that you screen out anyone with a serious contagious illness, there is no medical reason that your baby cannot have visitors or go visiting in her first weeks. On the other hand, you do want to avoid overstimulating her or overreaching your own level of energy. So weigh your choices carefully, be willing to say "no" whenever it seems like a good idea, and make your plans on a day-by-day basis. If you do go out, or have guests in, try to arrange the meetings in the morning when you and your baby are freshest.

Going Out

I can think of nothing designed to make new parents go crazy faster than to say that the baby has to remain indoors for four or six weeks. Cabin fever surely causes more problems to a new family than anything the great outdoors is likely to inflict. I tell my patients that, weather permitting, and with the baby appropriately dressed, they should go outside as soon as they feel up to it. However, it's a good idea to avoid crowds, not so much for the potential risk of infection but because of the overstimulation involved — no one will resist coming over to see the baby.

CHAPTER 4

Communication

Learning a New Language

During their first weeks together, parent and child are engrossed in learning a new, nonverbal language. In this language basic behavioral cues are the "words." The dialogue starts to become truly meaningful when the parent begins to sense in the child's behavioral cues specific messages and to respond to those messages with actions. The parent's ability to interpret the cues correctly is, obviously, critical to the continuing success of the dialogue, but so is consistency in the parent's response. In his own way, your baby notices; you might even say he keeps score. His first constructs in trust and positive expectations begin here. If his parents' responses are appropriate and consistent, the infant begins to feel that he has some control over what is happening to him. His hunger cry gets him fed, his Put-Me-Down cry results in the peace and quiet he wants, and his body language gets the lights turned down or the music turned off. This tells him that he is someone of worth and that he can depend on others to help him get where he wants to go. The parent is a big winner, too, for he or she can reasonably conclude from the child's growing competence that he or she is doing a good job. Parent and child are communicating and beginning to understand each other.

The process of learning each other's language is a gradual one. And it commences as soon as the baby is born, as demonstrated in the marvelous interactions that take place around something called the rooting response. Particular to newborns, this reflex can be seen when you stroke an infant's cheek and he automatically turns his face, mouth open, toward the stimulus. The traditional explanation of the rooting reflex is that it is a survival tool that exists to help the infant locate and latch onto his mother's nipple. This is not the whole story. Rather, the infant uses rooting to initiate a sequence in the cycle of behaviors and responses that we call nursing. Using filmed sequences to study nursing newborns, child psychologists have demonstrated that rooting does not directly contribute to the infant's ability to find the nipple. Rather, it elicits changes in the mother's behavior that end up providing the baby with better access to the nipple. She alters her body position, breast position, or moves the baby. To put it another way, nursing is something that mother and infant negotiate together as a team. This is true in many other instances, not just nursing. If you watch closely, you'll notice that it is often your infant who starts the sequence leading to mutual pleasure.

Because nursing is such an intimate, focused event for mother and child, it is to be expected that lots of other behavioral cues are exchanged at this time. Following is a compressed scenario of a typical "conversation" that might take place between an experienced infant and mother during a feeding. The baby is nursing contentedly. His body tone is good, his sucking a consistent burst-pause rhythm, his gaze locked on a button on his mother's blouse. Looking for more social interaction during nursing, she starts to talk to her child. Because talking right now threatens to break his concentration, which makes him feel uneasy, he closes his eyes and squirms a little, but continues nursing. Fortunately for the baby, mother has already figured out that this mild form of withdrawal — loss of eye contact — is her infant's way of saying "go back to the way things were before." She stops talking, and, almost immediately, the infant reopens his eyes and even starts gazing at her, making everyone feel good.

In a somewhat different scenario, with a mother who misreads the cue, or misses it altogether, the baby loses his concentration and begins to suck erratically and slap his hand against her breast. This sends a somewhat more forceful message to Mom. She will probably respond at this point, but will she respond appropriately? If she raises her voice to encourage her child to try harder, his sucking rhythm will deteriorate further, ending perhaps with the baby choking and totally detaching. Conceivably, the baby may take even more drastic measures if his messages are ignored or misinterpreted. He may clamp down on Mother's nipple. Her attention gained, albeit painfully, she stops nursing. If the infant is lucky, this may give Mom a moment to reflect on how the feeding went wrong and respond more appropriately. This time, perhaps, she whispers ever so quietly to him. He responds by opening his eyes, reaches for the nipple, reestablishes a sucking rhythm, and resumes nursing contentedly. Both have gained a sense of effectiveness and self-esteem that is the basis for making the relationship feel secure and worthwhile. The message is not just to respond, but parent and baby must respond appropriately to each other if they are going to learn this new language.

While messages or "words" are exchanged in the first few days, it takes at least six weeks, sometimes more than twelve, before parents and child begin to hold mutually satisfying "conversations" like these on a regular basis. But when they do, the relationship starts to bloom and the players truly begin to fall in love with one another. You might reasonably think that second-time parents could be quicker to develop a dialogue with a new baby than first-time parents. But in my experience, having done it once is not necessarily the best preparation for doing it again, and there may even be a disadvantage. Second-time parents often find it hard accepting the fact that each relationship is based on a unique dialect, that the behavior cues or "language" that was shared with their first child may have totally different meanings with their next. They also tend to forget that the experience of parenting has changed them in subtle ways, so that they are not the same with the second baby as they were with the first. Consequently, they tend to interpret their new baby's cues incorrectly.

When does communication start? I tell parents in prenatal counseling that they can expect to start getting messages from their baby as soon as she is born. Most of them laugh in disbelief, but when the great event arrives and they have their newborn in their arms, they begin to see what I'm talking about. The infant really does respond. Not all the time, but when she chooses to. Sometimes she prefers to shut down for reasons that seem puzzling or arbitrary at first. That's another piece of information that is hard to accept. Parents start out thinking they are going to control the situation, but here's this tiny baby with a mind of her own.

There's no sense throwing up your hands in confusion. You simply have to learn to read her cues — her cries, her smiles, her gaze, her body movements, and her muscle tone. That requires some basic understanding of what a baby's mind and body are capable of.

Physiology

When you are beginning to learn the newborn's language of body communication, some of the first discoveries are based on the changes you can see and feel in your baby's body.

People often think that a baby is cold, or perhaps has a heart problem, if his hands and feet are blue. That is possible, but the same changes occur, including blueness around the mouth, when the infant gets overstressed, overstimulated, or fatigued. Babies who are mad or agitated will get red in the face, or even over their whole body, just like the rest of us.

Another skin-color change is called mottling. This usually occurs on the arms and legs, sometimes on the body. The skin is often pale, with the appearance of vague, indistinct blue lines crisscrossing each other. The effect looks blotchy. This is another sign that your baby is dealing with more than she can cope with. Peraps there is too much activity around, the room is too noisy, the television too loud. Perhaps she has been played with for too long a time and needs a rest. It is another way for the baby to tell you that she wants a change.

Sometimes when you pick up your newborn you have your hand on his chest and you can feel his heartbeat. Or you notice his "soft spot," his anterior fontanelle, pulsing. Yes, it is fast, maybe 110 or 120 beats per minute. That is normal; when the baby is relaxed or asleep it may be 90. When he gets excited, and he's smiling or chirping at you, his heart rate will go up, even as high as 140 or 160 beats per minute. Like an adult, his heart rate may rise when he is stressed. But infants also tend to drop their heart rate in the same type of situation, often as low as sixty beats per minute.

The baby's breathing pattern is another clue. In the first few weeks, and sometimes thereafter, babies have periodic breathing — they breathe very fast, almost seem to pant, and then don't breathe again for ten seconds. Short periods of this are normal, especially when they are associated with going to sleep, at which time the baby goes back to her normal respiratory rate of twenty-two to thirty breaths per minute, perhaps a little slower if she is asleep. Like changes in skin color or heart rate, extended periodic breathing is a sign of stress, and the return to normal respiratory rate, with a smooth, even pattern, shows that the baby has compensated. Perhaps because you made the right move and turned off the television.

Physiologic changes are often easier for parents to read because they are linked together. You notice a change in body tone at the same time as you notice a change in color or respiratory rate. Physiologic changes are important because they are often early signals, which occur before some of the other types of communication discussed below. These early warning signals let you react appropriately, helping the baby stay on an even keel, so that he can use his other skills to be more responsive. Physiologic stability is a foundation for his other skills; if he is trying to compensate at the physiologic level, then he won't be able to use all his other marvelous social skills, which provide so much fun for both of you.

Let's look at an example. Tom was holding his four-week-old daughter, Anne. He had brought her in for a well-child visit. Tom was enchanted, and whenever Anne smiled, he would glow. He told me how he never expected to get this kind of response from her, and how much he despised the days when he had to be at work.

As he continued to talk with me and to play with her, I could see other changes in Anne. Her breathing rhythm was very erratic, and faster than normal. I could see that her hands were mottling, whereas they had been pink. I could see her soft spot pulsing — at what I guessed was about 140 or 150 beats a minute. Anne was trying to say "Cool it."

I could tell that Tom sensed a change, he was holding her a little farther away, not looking at her quite so much. When I asked him though, he didn't know what he was reacting to. He did take the suggestion to put her down, and she immediately looked at the white wall. In thirty or forty seconds, her breathing was normal and the mottling had disappeared.

Tom was intrigued. "Most of the time I keep going until she starts looking away or stares over my shoulder. Or else she flaps her arms and legs around and starts crying."

Tom has a new set of signals he can use. So can you.

Sight and Hearing

When I was in medical school, the experts and teachers were still not sure whether a newborn could see or hear in the first hours or days of life. Since then, we have come a long way in what we know about neonates, but still not far enough. And while the research continues, most parents are left to operate on old news. I constantly have parents repeat to me such old wives' tales as "Newborns can't really see," or "Babies only see shadows," or "Babies may be able to hear you, but they don't know where the sound is coming from," or "They can't distinguish one person's voice from another's, except maybe their mother's." I feel sorry for the parents who believe these old saws. They are missing so much.

We now know that a baby can see when he is in the uterus. Tested by means of ultrasound, a baby in the last trimester can be observed to turn in response to a light placed on his mother's abdomen. At birth, however, he sees through eyes that are not totally matured. It appears that his optimal focal range is limited to a few feet, making much of what he sees blurred, not unlike taking off the glasses you wear for distance vision. This is probably a form of protection, for it keeps him from seeing at least some of the visual stimuli that might tend to overload him or confuse his early efforts to understand the world around him. In any case, within close range he can see everything that matters to him, such as his mother's or father's face, his own hands, and the breast or bottle that nourishes him. A newborn baby's eyes can also pick out certain patterns, and some evidence suggests that among those patterns they are more drawn to look at a human face than any other image.

Even a person not privy to such data could clearly see by studying a baby for extended periods that the child is doing much more with vision than pediatricians or parents of a generation ago ever thought possible. When the baby is awake, not only will she look at your face, but she inspects very carefully different parts of your face. Most times she will look at your eyebrows or your hairline; perhaps the upper border of your glasses, if you wear them.

If your two-day-old baby is very calm and relaxed, he may establish eye-to-eye contact with you, but if you start talking he may look away or close his eyes. Don't try to force him to look back by shaking him or talking louder; that will only make him uncomfortable. By taking a positive approach, by treating your baby's cues as information rather than some kind of rejection, you will fare better and he will experience you as more responsive. For example, try moving your face farther away or stop talking and he will probably come back to looking at your face, if not your eyes. If you stop to think about it, what you are being asked to do is really no different from the way you would deal with an older child or an adult who looked away or pulled back in a social exchange. You would not further invade his space in the expectation of getting a warmer reaction; rather, you would pull back and look for other ways to encourage voluntary interaction. The fact that your infant can show you that he wants one kind of relationship at a particular time, but not another, should tell you just how sophisticated his system of communication is.

Sometimes Mom's change of makeup or her infrequent wearing of glasses will cause an infant to respond differently to her. So, too, Dad's growing of a beard can puzzle the baby into treating him like a stranger. And your baby will probably demonstrate marked likes and dislikes when it comes to objects, especially if she is prone to use visual fixation as a way of calming herself down. Studies show, for example, that within the first days of life babies are more likely to show an interest in patterns, sharply outlined figures, and moving objects than they are in plain or ambiguous shapes and surfaces, or stationary objects. Faces are generally best of all. But don't expect her morning preferences to be what your child wants to see in late afternoon when she is overstimulated.

Day or night, an infant's reaction to light will tell you something about how he is feeling and how responsive he is. Newborns generally do better with the lights turned down low, they keep their eyes open longer and they are most socially responsive. If you turn up the lights, your newborn will squint or close his eyes. Move from the shadow into the light while the baby is looking at your face, and she will often look away.

This shows that Baby does more than just see; she takes deliberate action based on that information. She takes the initiative. Not at six months, or at two years, but on her first day. While examining any one-month-old, I have come to expect that she will swivel her head and neck, often at an uncomfortable angle, in order to find a parent. (She would prefer to move her body, but she can't do that yet.) During the whole exam she will continue to look toward a parent. I don't know whether she can see the razor nick on her father's chin, or her mother's eyeshadow, but her insistence on watching the parent happens too often to be a coincidence.

Similarly, I expect the ten-week-old infant to be more socially responsive in the beginning of the exam if I talk with him from two feet away rather than from six inches away. If I do talk with my face right next to his, he usually will turn away and may start to cry. If parents doubt that the baby is controlling his own actions, I can usually persuade them with a simple demonstration: I talk with one of them while I put my face very close up to theirs, more or less nose to nose, and they invariably look away, too. Once parents see that their responses are identical to those of the infant, then it is easier to believe that the baby is controlling his own actions. And while examining the eight-week-old I have come to anticipate a different, one might say more mature, intentional choice. Rather than crying or fussing during the examination, the older baby is able to keep himself together by his own deliberate actions, for instance, picking a visual target, locking on to it, and using that to calm himself. He may try my face, a picture on the wall, my striped shirt, but chances are he will eventually settle on the white wall or ceiling and it will work to diffuse the stress he is feeling.

Which brings us to the subject of color. Many years ago investigators started to look at infants' perceptions of color and shape. The popular media has translated the findings to say that infants respond to bright colors the best, especially red. This is true, and not true. When infants are awake and organized, they often indicate a preference for a particular bright color. You will see them pick red, or yellow, or blue out of their surroundings and fix on something that color. But when they are disorganized, which is to say tired, hungry, or overstimulated, the reverse often happens. The same color that is a positive focus at 10 A.M. tends to be too much at 5 P.M. when the youngster is falling apart.

Just as babies can see before birth, they can also hear. On ultrasound it is possible to see the fetus move in response to certain sounds. Some researchers have proposed that the unborn baby is responding to rhythm only, but there is rather persuasive evidence that discrete sounds, albeit sounds muffled in a fluid environment, are also detected in the womb. Hearing tests performed on newborns indicate that at birth an infant can pick up a full range of sounds. And we know from measuring heartbeats that infants can also discriminate between intensities of sound, with the heart generally beating faster in the presence of louder sounds and slowing down in response to softer sounds. Within minutes of delivery the newborn can even associate sound with the direction it comes from, as shown by the way she turns her head toward the source.

With all this acuity, your newborn is likely to display marked auditory likes and dislikes. His choices will not necessarily be your choices for him. Just because you played Mozart or Billy Joel all through your pregnancy is no guarantee that he is going to find these sounds soothing now. For one thing, the music sounds different to him "on the outside" from the way it sounded "on the inside." Then again, he may not have liked it in utero, either. So as a parent you want to learn what your child likes to listen to, just as you learn what he likes to look at. And remember that even favorite sounds are not welcome all the time. Babies like peace and quiet, at least occasionally, just as much as the rest of us.

One of the favorite myths about babies is that they will *always* turn toward their mother's voice in preference to any other sound. Such a premise has its origins, I think, in the wish to have it so; it would certainly validate the mother's special place with her baby. The so-called scientific explanation often cited to support this contention is that the baby is born with a built-in familiarity with Mother's voice, having lived with it since way back in the fetal stage. But there are practical problems with that reasoning. What the baby heard while swimming in amniotic fluid is not the same sound by any means as the voice she now hears loud and clear. And if you present the newborn with two people talking, neither one of whom is his mother, the baby will generally turn toward whoever has the softer sound, the higher pitch, the generally more relaxed tone. Not infrequently, that person turns out, coincidentally, to be the mother, and the baby does indeed respond accordingly. But it is useful for the parent to recognize, once again, that the baby is exercising independent choice here and not reacting in some primal, instinctual way. Then again, babies are curious, and they may choose to turn toward a new voice purely because of its newness.

I would add one more thing about newborns and sound. At the end of the day, tired and fatigued, a four-week-old baby may respond with crying to any sound, or if he is not exhausted he may seem to calm down when you turn on the fan, the vacuum cleaner, or some other source of white noise. Actually, he may not be calming. More than likely he is simply habituating.

Habituation

As discussed in Chapter 3, Home From the Hospital, habituation is the ability to tune out. Responding appropriately to this behavior is one of the first opportunities that you have as a parent to show your infant that you understand her signals.

Communication involves more than just recognizing behaviors. Communication implies a feedback loop. If you respond to tuning out by lowering the stimulation level, this has to be very gratifying to the baby. As she struggles in the first weeks to cope with overstimulation, she will feel more relaxed and comfortable when her efforts are rewarded. On the other hand, she can't help but be more insecure if your response to her "sleeping all day" is to turn up the radio in order to try to make her get used to it.

Smiling and Facial Expressions

All babies can smile. As they get older, the meaning of smiles changes. The one day-old who smiles at you is saying that he feels good. It is not just the curve of the mouth that tells you he is smiling; the eyes look brighter, the eyebrows relax, and the wrinkles on the forehead disappear. Usually your baby will look directly at you and may establish eye-to-eye contact. His breathing will be smooth, and his body tone will feel good — he isn't tense, jittery, or limp. This does not happen automatically, and it does not happen because of gas. The baby is never going to smile for that reason. You wouldn't.

Young babies have complex emotions, and they express them the same way you and I do, on their faces. Sadness, curiosity, frustration, anxiety, satisfaction, anger, happiness — you will find them all if you just watch and recognize the obvious.

Once you get to know these expressions well, not just the broad outlines but the nuances, you will soon discover that the facial language of babyhood is not a transient phenomenon. Your infant's expressions are personal and permanent, and though his face will change as he grows up, his expressions remain essentially the same. The look of triumph on the face of the two-month-old who finds her fist and self-calms by sucking on it is not really very different from the look she will give you when she has learned to stand on her own at one, or ridden a bicycle for the first time without help at five or six. The look of defiance and demand, brows knit in a characteristic way, mouth set at a certain angle, that is visible on the face of the one-month-old wanting to be fed instantly, is not very different from the look you will see two years later when she is having a classic temper tantrum, or four years later when she is refusing to pick up her toys.

Sucking

Sucking is probably your infant's most common behavior, but within that behavior he has many variations. Besides sucking on a nipple, you will see him suck on his hand, his arms, his toes, his lips, and just about any other object available. Over the course of the first year, your infant will probably use sucking more often as a means to calm himself and to get organized than he will to feed, so you should think twice before thrusting a nipple in his mouth each time he begins to self-calm. Chances are you are probably going to frustrate him if you respond too quickly. Look at sucking as another form of communication and pay attention to the subtle cues.

The first time your newborn sucks on your finger or your nipple, her performance is likely to be inept. Her sucking is probably erratic. The baby's tongue gets in the way, or she frenetically grasps at the nipple and seems to swallow it. She spits, chokes, tries again, and then starts to fuss. Quickly, however, she improves her technique and with that develops a repertoire of sucking modes. Once you recognize the different patterns, you have another means of interpreting what is going on in your baby's mind and body.

For example, if the infant has had a rough day, then his sucking is likely to be uncoordinated — the rhythm may be irregular; the pressure may vary erratically. A smooth, even rhythm indicates that the baby feels fine and has plenty of energy reserves. And if the baby is just plain hungry, then the sucking is typically in a burst-pause pattern. With my own infant son, we came to know that whenever he sucked three or four times, then stopped for a few seconds, and then sucked three or four more times, he was telling us that he was hungry. Words could be no more precise than these signals.

Most infants have at least two different sucking rhythms that they use when trying to self-calm. The infant who can still manage to get herself under control fairly easily will suck at a very measured, deliberate pace, usually without any pauses, until she is sufficiently calm that she can engage in some other activity. The infant who is hanging on the ragged edge of disorganization or exhaustion may appear frantic. She fiercely grasps your finger or uses one hand to tightly hold the other in her mouth. The sucking is very fast-paced, very hard, often noisy. You wonder what will happen first: will she come up for air or swallow her elbow?

As her ability to self-calm improves, you will find that she sucks at an even pace more and more often. She will try different hand positions, too, starting on

the back of her hand, working around to her fingers
and thumb. While she is learning to self-calm, see if
turning down the lights, not talking, or possibly
changing her body position will help her along.

Body Tone and Motion

The newborn arrives with a minimal level of body and
head control. He starts improving on it, at least when
he is well-rested and alert, from that time forward, so
that what is normal in body tone for any given infant
is always evolving. Nonetheless, parents, without
knowing precisely how they do it, find that they soon
come to recognize what normal is and to use its presence or absence as a very sensitive indicator of when
their baby is feeling in control of himself and when he
is nearing exhaustion and disorganization.

One child may show that she is fatigued or overstimulated because she exhibits much more tremor —
very fine shaking motions of the hands, feet, and lips —
than normal. Another may suddenly look awkward,
with every movement exaggerated and inefficient for
the task at hand. Another becomes as limp as a rag
doll, or flails her arms and legs, or assumes a posture
with her arms extended, hands out, almost as if she is
trying to say "Stop!" In an effort to control herself, a
baby may even wrap her arms tightly across her chest,
almost as though she were giving herself a comforting
hug.

Loss of normal head control is another body signal
that an infant is on the edge of losing overall control,

as when the eight-week-old will no longer keep his head upright without your constant propping. And you may notice a change in the startle response, or Moro reflex, as it is technically known. Normally a stimulus like a sharp noise or having his head drop back slightly will cause the baby to startle, which is to say he stiffens, arches his back, and flings out his arms and legs. When a sudden change causes your infant to do this four or five times in a row, instead of once, he is losing control. The four-month-old who rarely startles when he is feeling well-rested, may do so frequently before he starts to cry.

Sleep-Wake Cycling

Changes in the baby's sleeping patterns are signals that parents often misinterpret. However, you should regard them as important whenever they occur. If, for example, your healthy one- or two-week-old daughter is not showing you any alert time in a 24-hour cycle, you can reasonably assume that she is overstressed. Similarly, the infant who changes from erratic catnaps to predictable two-hour naps, or longer, is telling you something positive. Either you are handling her and her environment better, or she has learned to self-calm and can now compensate for whatever stimuli were bothering her.

If you think about it, babies are not so different from the rest of us. As adults our sleep patterns vary because of fatigue, emotional changes, or stress produced by changing circumstances. So the four-month-old who has been sleeping wonderfully may sleep poorly the night after going to the family Fourth-of-July party; spending all afternoon putting on a show rather than taking his customary nap has left him off balance.

Sleep patterns change for social reasons — when is attention available? If 2 A.M. is the best available social time from her perspective, your baby will be up then. The one-year-old who starts to cry for you at night is often trying to express her independence. She isn't having separation anxiety. She doesn't like the limits of being in a crib. She wants to find out whether she has enough control to be able to get your attention at a time when she knows that you are not usually available. This is no different from her two-and-a-half-year-old sister, who demands a glass of water an hour after bedtime, or her five-year-old brother, who comes wandering out of the bathroom into your bedroom at 3 A.M. All of these changes are important signals. They don't just happen, and they don't just go away. They all underline the fact that social interaction is your child's highest priority.

Yawning, Sneezing, and Other Gyrations

The experts can't tell us for sure what makes us yawn. Sometimes it is a reflex response to inadequate oxygen intake, which is itself the result of shallow breathing, which may be caused by stress or inactivity. Sometimes we seem to do it because we are tired, but most of the time we yawn when we are bored or not paying attention (or the person next to us yawns, planting the desire to do the same). Infants probably yawn for the very same reasons — though one wonders what an infant has to be bored about, given the newness of his world. They also yawn for another reason: a yawn can be a request for change — a different face angle, a new tone of voice, less eye-to-eye contact. If you are interacting with your baby, and he suddenly yawns, think about what happened in the moments just preceding the yawn. Perhaps you raised your voice, maybe you changed his position, or a commercial came on the TV. He is reacting to a change, and usually requesting that you change back.

Sneezing serves much the same purpose. Infants *do* sneeze because of nasal secretions, dryness, or to clear their air passages, as do the rest of us. But many newborns and young infants will use sneezing as a means to get attention. And it is very common to see a five-month-old who has discovered that coughing, no matter how forced, will almost always turn heads. Yes, a five-month-old can manipulate you that way! Once again, look for something that happened just before the sneezing or coughing and ask yourself if your baby is trying to send you some kind of signal.

Finally, a baby can communicate by the act of pulling her legs up on her chest and crying. Admittedly, this may be a sign that the baby has stomach cramps. However, babies are just as likely to adopt this position when they are uncomfortable in some other way. If your child has had no signs of stomach problems, such as diarrhea, constipation, abdominal distention, or projectile vomiting, try to determine what else may have started the crying and look for ways to reduce that source of discomfort. Chances are she is mad because she has not been fed as soon as she wants, or she is too fatigued to get to sleep, or the three-year-olds playing in the next room are making too much commotion. Ironically, whatever the initial reason for crying, the infant swallows so much air that she gives herself a good case of gas, and then she has a second reason to cry. You can't do anything about the gas, and neither can she, once she has it. Maybe burping will help, but that is transient at best. The lesson, however, is to stop it before it starts. Perhaps you can do something about what precipitated the crisis, but the surest cure is for your baby to self-calm.

Eliciting: Starting a Social Conversation

A loving relationship is a very complex social system. It is sustained with messages and feelings that say "I love you" in countless different ways. To be most satisfying, both parent and child must participate equally, in what Berry Brazelton and Heidi Als have called an intricate dance. In this dance each partner must have his turn at leading and following.

Too often parents inadvertently get in their baby's way; they want to lead the dance all the time, or they become impatient when the baby does not respond as quickly and as fully as they want her to. They push and prod, trying to stimulate her into some kind of interaction, which only causes her to withdraw more. The more she signals that she cannot tolerate their advances through changes in body tone, tremor, or eye aversion, the more determined they become to elicit a social conversation and the less likely their child is to respond favorably. She may even shut down all together.

This is not to say that the child can't respond. She will, but in her own good time, and when she can play a part in directing how the interaction will go. Before that time, which is to say before the infant can call on self-calming skills, she is always at risk of being overwhelmed by overeager parents, and she knows that. Later, when she can self-calm, parents may still find that a direct approach (walking into a room, right up to the child, who is calmly gazing out the window, and saying "Hi") gets a turn-off signal. The infant looks away. She is not ready, and she would rather be left alone. The thing to do is to try again later, or try a different approach, and see how she responds then.

You can help your child as he learns social skills by concentrating on just one facet of communication at a time — eye contact, perhaps, or voice contact, or touch. It may sound difficult, particularly if you are impatient for lots of feedback from your child. But it is the only sure way to build a mutually satisfying relationship. In being dealt with sensitively and patiently, the infant can gain a sense of confidence, and he in turn will reward you with longer and longer periods of interactive play. Eventually, all the separate skills will come together into a smoothly integrated dance, but it may take days and weeks of practicing each of the steps.

To see how a parent and child might work their way through one of the steps, let's take a look at Bob and his new son, Mark, as they explore each other's limits through eye-contact "games." Mark is now six weeks old, and while Bob has been excited over being a parent, so far he has felt a certain lack of engagement in Mark's affairs. Part of the problem, as he sees it, is that Mark is being breast-fed. His wife, Mary, suggested last week that Bob try giving the baby a bottle when he comes home from work each evening, but they quickly realized that Mark is just too frantic at that time of day for either father or son to benefit. So now, Bob has rearranged his schedule at the office so that he can go to work a little later and give Mark a bottle in the morning. This turns out to be better for everyone. With Bob in charge, Mary gets some needed extra sleep, and father and son get some concentrated time alone when Mark is at his best.

Within a few days, Bob learns to adjust his manner of handling Mark in the morning based on how well Mark has slept during the preceding night. Some nights he sleeps in three-hour blocks and refuses to go back to sleep until Mary has nursed him. Then he wakes in a groggy, grumpy mood and wants as little interaction as possible while taking his bottle. Other nights Mark puts himself back to sleep without a feeding — he is beginning to learn self-calming but results are still erratic — and those are the mornings, Bob knows, when Mark seems most responsive.

Even on good days, though, there are things Mark will not tolerate just now. Mark is habituating less and less, and as a result the sound of radio or TV that he ignored two weeks ago now seems to drive him crazy. If Bob so much as talks to Mark while he is taking his bottle, he is likely to get distracted and disorganized. But there is one kind of stimulation that Mark can handle when he is alert and well rested: he tends to be visually curious. Indeed, ever since Bob began spending more one-on-one time with his son, he has been amazed at Mark's visual curiosity. Mark often stops feeding just to look around. Bob never expected that from a baby! Bob has thought to himself that when Mark is ready to make a social connection, the first overtures will probably come by way of his visual curiosity.

Bob is excited today, for he senses that everyone is off to a particularly good start. Mark has had a good night, sleeping seven hours without a feeding. At least twice during that time he awoke, but Mark managed to self-calm and put himself back to sleep. Bob knows because the sound of his sucking was loud enough to wake his parents! Now he has taken five ounces of expressed breast milk quickly. His sucking is smooth and his body tone normal. Bob is tempted to look at him or talk to him, but yesterday that seemed to upset Mark. Now Bob is making a point of being very quiet as he holds the bottle and reads the newspaper propped beside him. Still, he senses that Mark is looking at the 'side of his face.

When Mark is done, he puts the baby in his infant seat on the table so that father and son are positioned alongside each other, their faces on the same level. Bob waits. Mark takes only a few seconds before he is staring intently at the side of Bob's face. Bob turns ever so slightly to look at him, his face still at an angle, and smiles. Mark smiles back. Bob slowly comes full face to Mark. Mark grins, and then turns his face away a little. Bob doesn't move, and Mark partially closes his eyes and tightens his brow. Bob looks away, Mark's face relaxes, and he turns his head back toward his father. Bob waits, and then turns his face back to Mark. Mark continues to look at him. Bob makes a face at Mark. (What Bob thinks of as his "goon" face is destined to be something private between father and son, a bit of foolishness that he is too embarrassed to reveal when Mary is around.) Mark chirps. Bob makes more faces. Mark grins more. Bob feels foolish and looks away. Mark bats his hands and squirms in his chair to get Bob's attention. Bob looks back, and Mark bursts into a huge smile. Feeling triumphant, Bob claps his hands, says "Great, Mark," and laughing, starts to rise from his chair. He wants to get Mary so she can share his pleasure.

This is too much for Mark. He looks away and starts to cry, trying to get his hand to his mouth. Bob immediately realizes that he has overstepped Mark's bounds, and settles back down in his chair quietly. He tries to help Mark get to his own fingers, but then realizes that Mark sucks on the back of his hand, not his fingers. Ever so gently he changes the position of Mark's hand. His son starts sucking, maintaining a fixed gaze over Bob's shoulder as he does so. When Mark is calm once again, Bob moves a little closer and waits for Mark to look at him. It takes about twenty seconds, and then when Mark turns to him, he knows his son is ready. Just then Bob hears a noise behind him and glances away. Mark isn't prepared for that, and protests by kicking his feet. Bob immediately turns back. Mark again cracks a big smile. Bob smiles at him. Mark continues to look like the cat who swallowed the mouse, and Bob whispers, "Pleased with yourself, aren't you? Kick your legs and you get instant attention." From the twinkle in his eye, Mark all but says "Yes." Bob realizes that this will go down in his book as an unforgettable morning. Not only has Mark really smiled at him for the first time, and shown himself able to get his father's attention by his own means, but the two of them are "talking" to each other. Whispering actually, and Mark is still looking at him. They have crossed a major boundary—doing two things at once.

Bob whispers a few more things about the joys of being a father and tries some more new faces over the next ten minutes. Then he notices that Mark's lip is beginning to quiver a little, and he is sucking pretty forcefully on his hand. He decides that it is probably time to quit. He moves Mark's seat around so that he can look out his favorite window, wondering whether the baby really sees the flowers out there or is just taking a visual break, and goes to the stove to see if he can do a little better at not making the fried eggs quite so crunchy this morning.

Both father and son feel good, for both have established a new level of communication. Over time, as they gain experience with each other, their repertoire of behavioral cues and positive responses will continue to expand, leading in turn to more and more satisfying levels of communication.

As parents realize that their infant can initiate eye contact and can give them predictable signals about how they should respond, then the playtimes between them become longer, more spontaneous. As the baby gains more competence at self-calming and more confidence in the appropriateness of his parents' responses, he maintains contact and initiates contact. The parent, no longer limited to one aspect of social interaction, such as vision, can now experiment with new ways of interacting with the child.

A similar sequence takes place with voice contact, which the infant may want to explore as a separate activity at first. But voice can gradually be mixed with eye contact, touch, and motion as the baby's signals indicate that she can tolerate, even welcome, more. Every parent can remember the first time he or she made mutually-agreed-upon contact with a baby in a comfortable and relaxed manner. That thrill, however, pales beside the thrill of being able to pick up your child and say hello to a smile freely and *intentionally* given just to you.

This positive relationship can only emerge through your learning about and responding appropriately to each other. To achieve this the baby is responsible for developing readable behavior cries, which the parents must recognize. They cannot be responding to some idealized dream, what Grandmother says should happen, or an opinion given in a book. Parents also need to learn about their own behaviors. For instance, smiling when you are angry with your child is misleading and ambiguous. Equally important is the ability to make decisions in a way that will give your child a predictable, appropriately responsive world to rely on.

As the infant becomes more assured that his responses have predictable effects on his parents, the behavioral language of the relationship expands dramatically. It is this understanding that helps parents learn what the different cry messages mean. Without this knowledge of the cry messages and the infant's other behaviors, it is difficult to help the baby learn to self-calm and to encourage him to expand those skills. Thus behavioral language, crying communication, and self-calming make it possible to set a schedule, and play time becomes the free, open, and exhilarating experience that everyone wants so much. After the chaos and exhaustion of the first weeks, this makes having a baby finally seem worth it all.

CHAPTER 5

Crying

Completing the Baby's Behavioral Language

Specific cries have specific meanings. In the first few
months of life this message system serves as a way for
parents to understand both the basic needs of their infant as well as the child's emotions. It augments the
behavioral language made up of the baby's nonverbal
cues and messages. Later, during the second year, as
the child begins to use words, crying becomes exclu-
sively an emotional outlet and a way to manipulate the
feelings of others.

Developing a repertoire of cries takes time. Your baby,
by the time she is four months old, may have developed as many as a dozen different cries to deal with a
multitude of needs and feelings. But at birth these different cries are not clear because she is inexperienced
in interpreting her situation. The specific messages are
not there, so there is no consistent difference in tone
or cadence that lets you really distinguish one cry message from another.

Consider how limited her experience is at birth. In
the uterus she was fed constantly — hunger was un-

known to her. Thirty minutes after delivery, she may well feel uncomfortable and in need of soothing, but she does not yet know what is happening around her, what she likes or dislikes, whether the soothing is best obtained by being held, being talked to, being rocked, being swaddled, being fed, or being placed in a more appealing environment than the bright lights, noise, and hurried activity of the hospital. All that remains for her to discover and for her to communicate once she has evolved a message system. A great deal has to happen in the next few weeks for all these parts to fall into place.

Many new parents leave the hospital without ever having heard their baby cry, except perhaps at the delivery. When you do hear him cry, don't expect to be able to make any sense of it at first. For the baby to use crying as communication requires a considerable amount of practice and interaction with his care-givers, and that takes several weeks. Meanwhile, what you hear is an indecipherable code of whimpers, cries, moans, and fussing, as he tries to accustom himself to a new and confusing world.

Here's how one parent describes her initial encounter with her baby's crying:

"The first time I heard Caitlin cry was when we put her in the car seat for the ride home. I didn't know whether she was crying because she was uncomfortable, scared, or just disgruntled. We sat in the parking lot and did everything that we could think of to quiet her, but nothing worked. So we drove home with a crying baby. In retrospect I think that she was disoriented and saying 'What the hell is going on now?'

Of course we felt we were immediately failing as parents. I was in tears by the time we got home."

And another mother reports:

"I expected him to cry all day after the circumcision. But it didn't seem to bother him anywhere near as much as being the baby chosen by the nurse to show us new mothers on the maternity wing how to give a bath. That told me I had a lot to learn about what bothers a baby."

Once at home the parents' prime concern is to identify when the baby really needs them and what they, as parents, need to do. The task is not just to stop the crying, but to identify what message is contained in that cry. Don't get discouraged.

"I was very proud of myself. I thought that I was really doing well. I was sure that I could identify when Rachel needed to be changed and when she needed to be fed. There were other cries which I did not understand, but I felt that I was ahead of the game. But I'll never forget that afternoon when she was sixteen days old. The cry sounded the same at 3 P.M. as at 11 A.M. I was sure that she was hungry. But she just wouldn't nurse. She didn't need to be changed. She wouldn't go to sleep. She definitely was upset, but I had no idea why."

Learning what the cries mean is a matter of "parent education." Like many other areas of the relationship, this is an interaction. The baby initiates with a sound, but the parent's reaction partially shapes the meaning. If every cry is heard as a need to be fed, then the infant's communication system is limited. On the other hand, the parent who experiments and tries numerous different responses opens new avenues of communication.

You will learn what your baby is trying to say more quickly if you begin from a premise that your child is trying to provide some message through his cries. Rather than guessing at the message, which is likely to cause your responses to be inappropriate and confusing much of the time, start with a relatively low-level response, and then slowly build your involvement until the crying stops, indicating that you have met your child's need. A typical sequence might go as follows:

1. Talk to the baby from across the room.

2. Go over to the baby and rub the child's back.

3. Roll the baby over and talk from a closer range.

4. See if the baby will suck on his own hand or your finger.

5. Check to see if the baby needs to be changed.

6. Pick the baby up and walk over to a chair.

7. Talk to the baby again.

8. Again try letting the baby suck on his hand or your finger.

9. Feed the baby.

Each step increment of response increases your level of involvement. At the same time, your baby is offered a variety of different responses to choose from. If the baby stops crying when you rub her back, for example, then a back rub is all that is required on this particular occasion. If, on the other hand, she is really hungry, then all of the steps leading up to being fed will not stop her crying, and you will end up feeding her. But not because the clock told you to, even though it was four hours after the last feeding. The whole procedure from step one to step nine takes no more than a minute or two. And it conserves the parent's energy. If you don't know now why that matters, you will by the end of the first month.

Of course, most people say "Feed the baby," when he cries. Initially, this will almost always look like the right response, except perhaps with the extremely fatigued or overstimulated infant. Why? Because feeding meets all of the baby's priorities except sleep. Feeding provides the baby with all the possible soothing behaviors, including touch, warmth, sucking, rhythmic stimulation (such as rocking), social stimulation, and food. But consider how excessive the response is if, in reality, the baby simply wants to be talked to and the parent responds by feeding the child: it is like the baby asking for a quarter and the parent giving him a twenty-dollar bill and telling him to keep the change. For a while, the baby may be placated, but the parent soon goes broke. The physical and emotional demand is too high to sustain. And no communication is established. Regardless of the message, the baby always gets the same response.

Here is how some new parents resolved this question of when to feed the baby:

"It was easy to be paranoid about weight. All that everyone asked about was whether Alex was getting enough to eat. How much weight had she gained since yesterday and did I weigh her after every feeding to make sure that she had enough? How much was enough, anyway? There was no way to tell from the hospital; they always fed her on a schedule. How was I supposed to know when she was hungry, or what was enough?"

"When Sharon cried, I always checked my watch. If it was more than two hours since her last feeding, then I'd assume that she needed to be fed. In the prenatal class and the breast-feeding class, they said that was always the first thing to do. By the end of one month I felt that motherhood meant never doing anything else besides nursing her. Frankly, I was disappointed. I was not having fun. I wanted to be more to her than a refillable milk container."

"I had nightmares about the pictures of the Gerber baby. I did not want Justin to be fat; I have had weight problems all of my life, and I don't want that for him. But he seemed to want to eat all of the time. I could tell from the rolls of fat on his thighs that he was getting enough, so how could he be hungry all the time? Nevertheless, every night for seven weeks, whenever he cried, I dutifully pulled myself out of bed — another two hours, another feeding. One night I was mad, exhausted, but for some reason still rational. As soon as I picked him up, Justin quieted. I didn't have to nurse him at all. He fussed when I put him down, but I wasn't interested in playing. It took a minute or two before he found his hand to suck, and then he went back to sleep. That was the last night I got up. There have been many nights since then when I've heard him awake in there — times when I used to go feed him. Sometimes I can hear him sucking on his hand, sometimes he talks himself back to sleep, and sometimes I don't know what he does, because I don't get up. Most nights I sleep through, except when his chattering is too loud. And he's no longer fat. He slimmed down very nicely."

"I hadn't talked to Rose, my college roommate, since before I was pregnant. She was excited to hear about David and how he was doing. We were laughing and excited just like back in school, and then David started to cry. Rose could hear him: I was hesitating, not really listening to her anymore. Shortly she suggested that she call back another time. I hesitated, and then promised I'd call her. We both laughed — each one of us thinking that it would be another year.

"As we hung up, I realized I had slammed down the phone. Neither one of us understood why we couldn't talk longer, except that David was crying. She wanted to be a mother, she wanted to hear what all of this was like, except the crying, of course. I wished that I was in her shoes — about to go out for lunch. After six weeks of this I was fed up, pardon the pun, constantly being at his beck and call. But I gave up a great job to be a mother, and I was going to be a good one.

"All these thoughts took about a minute, maybe two. It wasn't until I reached his room that I realized he wasn't crying anymore. I stopped at the door to listen.

He was loudly smacking on his hand. I felt somewhat relieved because I thought that meant he was hungry. But as I walked in the room I was puzzled. He was very relaxed and content. His eyes were half shut; he was clearly going back to sleep.

'So much for hunger,' I thought to myself. Suddenly that day I started to 'hear' a lot more. There were many reasons for David to get upset and food wasn't always the answer, and neither was I. I could see that he felt better when I recognized his cries; and I sure did. There were times when I could talk with Rose, and other times when he needed my help and I couldn't.

"No one was more surprised than Rose when I called her back ten days later. But now the story I had to tell her was different than what it would have been before. I could tell her how I felt and what I did. But I wasn't angry anymore. We were able to talk for an hour, and David spent the whole time sucking on his own hand and looking out the window. He kept himself calm and under control without any help from me. Both Rose and I were impressed."

"Something serious had to be wrong when, for the third day in a row, John couldn't be calmed by nursing at 5 P.M. I thought that maybe he was sick or that it was something I had eaten, but the rest of the day he had been fine. Five to nine, however, was murder. Nothing worked. I finally put him down and shut off the light. He was quiet in less than a minute. I was so happy, for me and for him. He did it himself. I started to think about him differently. He was a real person. He needed my help, but he didn't need me all the time and he didn't need to be nursed all the time. And I started to have a better relationship with him."

Crying is certainly more than "exercise for the lungs." Like older people, babies do cry for a reason. You can't hear the messages unless you accept the basic notion that babies really do have feelings and needs that they can tell you about if you are willing and able to listen. Learning how to listen and learning what the messages mean is not just a matter of responding indiscriminately every time the baby cries; your baby needs appropriate responses. Nor are you going to "hear" because of some kind of loving parental instinct. There is real skill to interpreting a baby's messages, developed through experience and observation.

There are no universal cries. You learn about your own child. For instance, one baby who is hungry may cry in a way that sounds very different from another infant. For most children, volume is not a reliable indicator. My son's most abrasive, difficult-to-listen-to-cry was when he was hot, followed closely by the cry when he wanted to be put down. The pitch for "Put Me Down" was very shrill, for "Hot" even higher. The tone for both cries was insistent, and he would hold long bursts of noise before taking a breath. The cadence could be represented as follows: (———— ... ———— ...) where the dots are breath pauses and the dashes crying.

For "Put Me Down" and "Hot" he would move his arms and legs vigorously, whereas when he was hungry he had less body motion and would make more attempts sooner to start sucking on his hand. He rarely would self-calm when he was hot; he never had tears when he was hungry. The hungry cry had a lower tone, the cadence was short bursts, short breaths. When he was tired, he would cry with slightly longer bursts than when he was hungry, with a plaintive tone.

In representative code,

Put Me Down looks like (——— ... ——— ... ———)

Hunger looks like (— ... — ... — ...)

Tired looks like (—— ... —— ... —— ...)

If he was mad, he would get red in the face and repetitively, demandingly kick his right leg. On waking up, he sounded just like the cat. Then there were his attention cries — at least four variations — during which he would usually be smacking his hands on a surface or waving them in the air, and the instant smile when I turned or spoke to him, or the dog came running, was the giveaway for what the cry meant.

You learn by listening to tone, pitch, and cadence, and perhaps by watching other behaviors, like body motion or skin color. Perhaps you literally want to take crib notes to help yourself, your spouse, your babysitter, or Grandmother. Some people even try tape recorders. Use whatever will help you learn fastest — it's to everybody's benefit.

Certain babies do not have as many cries as others, so their messages are more ambiguous, their needs somewhat harder to satisfy explicitly. Some take a longer time to figure out what they want and how to "say" it.

"My relationship with Tommy got off to a bad start. I think that part of the problem was in my determination to build trust at any cost. I was convinced that if I didn't respond to him as soon as he cried, he wouldn't trust me. But by the fifth week he seemed to think he was entitled to my instant response, regardless of the time of day or night. That wasn't trust. That was mother abuse."

"Crying is just crying to my mother. She never learned any other language besides English. She insists that all you have to do is get a baby on schedule, and that she was able to do this with me and my sister by the time we were three weeks old! Maybe she did, and maybe she didn't, but the underlying message of her argument is that we should be in control of the baby. So long as I took my guidance from her, I was bound to feel like a failure as a father. Some part of me said this was ridiculous. That phone conversation with you helped me and my wife relax a lot. We began to see that Jimmy really was trying to tell us something, but that he hadn't yet figured out how to do it. And we hadn't figured out how to translate for him either. I can honestly say that we communicate very well, now, but it has taken weeks to get there."

"I probably spoiled Ryan, my first baby. Every time he cried I went running, and because I heard all cries as identical, I tended to deal with all of them the same way. How confusing that must have been for him. How insensitive I must have seemed when he was telling me he wanted to be held one time and fed another and played with another and all I ever did was stick a bottle in his mouth. I know Brendan, our second child, much better in this regard. I can recognize in him six or seven different cries, and everything goes along more smoothly. He sleeps better than Ryan did at his age, and he behaves better, too."

The First Few Months: What to Do about Fussing

"Andy would grunt and groan and squirm around in his crib. To me it looked as though he were crying, but he never really started to cry out loud until I picked him up. That made me start to see the difference between fussing and crying."

"I was getting up at 2 A.M. with Lena. I could rock, talk, nurse, sing, or walk her, but nothing mattered one way or the other. We'd be up together for two hours, both of us exasperated and exhausted. It was only when you asked me to tell you exactly what she was doing when I would go into her room that I realized she wasn't crying. Since I expected her to be crying each time, that is what I heard. Now I realize that her 2 A.M. routine is fussing. If I leave her alone, she generally goes back to sleep on her own. If she starts to cry, then I try to listen for what the message is. Then I can decide what I need to do."

"I've learned that when Kate starts fussing, there is nothing I can do to help her. She will either calm herself down or move on to crying. It's surprising, but it's easier to deal with the crying. In each episode of fussing there's always an important lesson I can learn about the daily routine or the way I just gave her a bath or the fact that the visitors stayed too long. Once I see the point, then I can make changes in how I handle things in the future. That is a nice feeling — it's like we are a team working together."

"My mother-in-law is a great person, but she is too much for the twins. As soon as one of them starts to fuss it is like a warning light. If I don't separate them from her, we face a sure catastrophe. She likes to talk. She's very lively. They just can't take it right now, and rather than having them blow up, and get me angry, and have her feel rejected, I act quickly and get them off to a quieter place. Fortunately, she's very understanding and she now is likely to pick up on trouble brewing almost as fast as I do and pull back on her own."

"Whimpering is a lot like fussing for Carolee. It used to be a signal that I needed to do something different. If I didn't, the whimpering was sure to become a cry. Many times I just changed the radio channel or put her in her chair. Recently though she has begun to use whimpering differently at night than she does during the day. At night it is almost always a signal that she is OK. She gets herself back to sleep. During the day, whimpering is a sign that she is in a transition zone. Sometimes I can make an adjustment that will help. But as she has gotten better at calming herself, more and more she does it on her own without my help. That's nice in the day or night."

Gas: Cause or Effect?

Nothing associated with crying causes more confusion and misreading than your baby's bouts of intestinal gas. If the baby is not hungry, then the local experts will always offer a convincing case that your child is crying on account of gas. Of course, by that time the baby has been crying for fifteen minutes and generally has swallowed enough air that gas *is* a major problem. Indeed, once a baby is suffering from the discomforts of gas, a vicious cycle of fussing, crying, more air swallowing, and more gas starts operating, and neither you nor your baby can do much to stop it except wait for exhaustion to set in. But always keep in mind that gas is probably secondary to something else. To treat the gas with paregoric or some other medication but fail to look for the underlying cause is like treating a fever without treating the infection.

You can deduce the cause of crying-related gas best by judging the context of the situation. Take, for example, the common circumstance of the infant who is inconsolable at 5 P.M. He cries so long and so loudly every day at this time that someone will tell you he surely has colic. But what is probably going on is overload. The baby has been out in the stimulus-filled world for a lot of hours by this time of the day, and now as you swing into action putting away groceries, preparing dinner, doing the laundry, or just catching up with other members of the family, your baby is reaching his threshold of tolerance. He starts to fuss and fidget. As a result, he is rapidly developing a major case of gas and starts complaining about it. The fussing becomes crying. If he could self-calm, perhaps he could escape all this, but he hasn't learned how yet.

Certain children also develop gas because of the way they suck. This is frequently true in the first five or six weeks when the baby may be very frantic or uncoordinated or erratic in sucking — with the result that he swallows a lot of air. Gas can also develop as the result of intolerance toward milk sugar (lactose) or certain proteins contained in the milk, but this is relatively rare. The best indicator of such an intolerance is accompanying diarrhea or other signs of difficulty, such as the baby seeming hungry, but refusing to eat more than an ounce or two and then quickly developing cramps or gas. Feeding small infants solid food before they can digest it properly will also produce gas. Following are some verbal snapshots of how parents in my practice came to grips with this particular feature of crying behavior.

"I was convinced that Tracy must have a serious stomach problem. Every afternoon she began crying in a really miserable way, as though she had gas. Someone suggested giving her paregoric, but I hated that idea; I had taken no drugs during my pregnancy and delivery, and now I was supposed to give her some kind of narcotic? No way. She was just two weeks old! So we tried changing her formula — three times, with no apparent effect. Then I noticed that she never had gas in the morning. Perhaps it was coincidental, but most often Tracy began to cry around the time when Kenny got home from nursery school; in fact she often began on the ride to pick him up. I couldn't make any direct connection at first, because Kenny was so good with her. But I had to admit, she handled car rides at other times just fine. As an experiment, I asked a friend to go pick Kenny up after school and keep him for an hour, until Tracy's nap time. The first day was a smashing success. The fussing stopped. I saw that to cure her gas I had to keep her and Kenny apart in the afternoons. His rambunctious good spirits were just too much for her at this age."

"Some days I would nurse Gavin easily, but other days he would fuss and his stomach would complain with loud rumbles as though he had a painful gas condition. At night, though, and early in the morning, everything was always fine. I thought my own eating habits were the problem, so for ten days I stayed away from pizza and chili and coffee and just about everything that had real taste. But nothing changed. Gavin was still on-again, off-again with his feedings during the day and perfect at night. Then, it dawned on me, there *was* a pattern after all. Just about every time during the day that he nursed comfortably, we were sitting in the basement playroom, where it is cooler, quieter, darker, and out of traffic — the same general atmosphere as the nighttime feedings in the nursery. Almost every time he had a bad nursing session it was in the living room. Usually, I would have the TV going. Maybe he doesn't like the same soap operas I do! Anyway, I try to nurse Gavin in quieter surroundings now, and when a feeding coincides with my TV time, and we are in the living room after all, I turn the lights down and listen through an earpiece so he doesn't have to hear it. And, yes, I've gone back to eating spicy foods again, thank heavens."

"My mother tells me that when she was nursing me, I had gas constantly. The doctor blamed it on an allergy to breast milk, so she had to stop nursing. So you can bet that when Jeffrey started fussing after feedings, I thought, 'Here we go again.' But certain things I noticed made his situation seem different. For one thing, he never had gas after his first and biggest feeding in the morning. For another, he didn't have diarrhea. The more I thought about it, in fact, the more I was able to associate the bouts of gas with those feedings in which he appeared frenetic or agitated. I could tell because he would change his sucking rhythm. He was swallowing more air in the process and this was where the gas was coming from. I just needed to learn not to put him in situations where he got so worked up. That helped, but there were still transitions late in the day that he couldn't handle. The 'gas cries' really ended as he learned to calm himself down and he was able to cope with those situations himself."

"We tried the drugs — Mylicon drops, Bethanecol, paregoric, and many others. We even tried soy formula instead of breast milk. Angie still fussed. She was miserable. Then you suggested feeding her in the dark and not interacting with her. She stopped having gas by the second feeding. That was when she started to smile, too. What a bonus!"

"Evan had gas on Tuesday and Thursday and Friday afternoons. At first it wasn't clear why Monday and Wednesday were OK. Then I realized that I played bridge on Tuesday and took him to exercise class at the end of the week. Too much chatter and too many changes, obviously. He would start to fuss every time, and then he would get gas, and it was all over for the afternoon. By getting a baby-sitter and having him stay home for those hours, I was able to cure his gas problem."

The Baby Who Does Not Cry

To the parents whose baby suffers with interminable fussing or recurrent episodes of gas pains, the notion of an infant who does not cry can sound pretty wonderful. These noise-weary folks would give anything for a quiet baby, or at least so they think. But strange to say, parents of "non-criers" often get to a point where they would welcome some good old-fashioned wailing and screaming. Not only do they worry that something is physically wrong with their baby (it rarely is), but they also lack cues as to what is going on with their child.

As in the case of "gas," quietness alone is rarely an indication of a more serious underlying problem; there have to be other symptoms, as well, such as abnormal body tone, unusual sleeping patterns, delayed motor development, and consistently low levels of social response to indicate a physical or neurological problem of consequence. Certainly, the parent of a non-crier who feels uneasy should check with the baby's physician. Generally speaking, however, the non-crier is just doing a remarkably good job of habituating. The quiet may end abruptly during the second month, and you and your non-crier will suddenly discover her vocal cords.

The silence does, unfortunately, create communications problems for parent and child, however, because the baby may not seem to be as interesting or as interested as the more expressive child. This is an unfortunate impression. Some children are not habituating, and they do not "change" at two months. These children are often remarkably organized and self-sufficient. They simply don't cry much. Here's how some parents in my practice worked their way through this period:

"For the first nine or ten weeks after Robbie was born, I didn't feel like a mother in some ways. Robbie would often be awake for long periods of time, and he was quite happy, but he required very little. He was content to be fed whenever I felt like it, and I could change his diaper whenever I pleased. Nothing ever seemed to matter too much to him. If he hadn't been so pleasant about it, and awake so much, I would have felt that he was retarded. Still, I was anxious, too, because he didn't need me, and sometimes I would wake at night wondering what would happen if he was really in trouble. Would he let me know? Was I doing something that was just basically wrong? Did he hate me? I had never heard of a baby who cried so little. Looking back after two other kids, I can see how "easy" Robbie was, but I worried constantly then. I used to smile when he would cry because then I would feel needed."

"What saved us both with Maria, who never cried, was that I gradually learned how to read other signals. For example, the color in her face and how she was moving her arms and legs told me what she was feeling or what she wanted. And the way she sucked on her fist — fist clenched sucking on her knuckles or whole hand in her mouth — was a clue to whether she was hungry or just excited. I never knew whether she slept through the night or not, because she didn't make a sound, but I slept 'like a baby.'"

"The thought was always in my head that perhaps Frankie can't cry. Maybe he won't be able to talk. I constantly wondered about the delivery — when the doctor had to suck the meconium out of his trachea maybe they damaged his vocal cords. Now he's a total chatterbox. I hope that his personality stays the same. Nothing ever ruffles him. He is one of the nicest kids I have ever met!"

Building Trust

By following the sequence of parental responses described on page 134 and paying attention to how the baby responds, you can gradually sort out your baby's crying vocabulary. As your responses become more and more accurate, your child learns to trust you and the predictability of her personal world. The four-week-old may be satisfied at being fed every time she cries, because feeding coincidentally takes care of a multitude of needs, but the four-month-old is more discriminating and wants her communications dealt with more appropriately. If her crying is intended to say "Pay attention to me" or "Play with me," then having you come at her with applesauce is frustrating, not to say disappointing. By watching, listening, and learning from your baby, you can save your energy for more valuable tasks while the child gains a greater feeling of control.

This is a major part of building trust in the relationship. For both the parents and the child, the object is not just how fast to stop the crying, but who does what to stop the crying. With greater understanding, you decide what you actually need to do to respond to each kind of situation, and exactly how much the child can do. For instance, he learns how to wait to be fed, how to put himself back to sleep. Conversely, you discover what the cry sounds like when he's mad or really in distress.

Don't expect to rationalize each response so precisely that you can get it right without practicing. More often than not, each situation becomes practice for doing it better the next time. And that holds true for both you and your baby. You will find that you help the baby acquire new skills and that she is more resilient. Her competence is valuable to both of you. By fostering her autonomy you spend less time waiting on her and more time enjoying the relationship. The greater the number of messages, and the more predictable your responses, the smoother family life will be.

What Can Babies Learn to Say?

Every baby's crying repertoire is unique. Some infants develop half a dozen effective messages within the first six or eight weeks, other children have ten or twelve different signals before the third month of life. Most new parents understandably hear distress in all these messages, but with the exception of pain and hysterical crying, most cries are not so much cries of distress as expressions of some very practical concerns for which crying is the only available vocabulary. Specific meanings are distinguishable not so much by loudness as by cadence, tone, pitch, and the context in which they are delivered.

These messages include:

frustration

anger

hunger

fatigue

desire to be changed

desire to be put down

overstimulation

pain

sleep/wake transitions

hysteria

disorganization/confusion

Most children also have distinguishable cries that demand different levels of physical affection or social play:

light touch

being talked to without holding

talking, social play without being held

being held quietly

total play — which involves being held, smiling, talking, all at once

As you and your baby establish an ever-more-reliable pattern of interchanges, as you literally get to know each other, you lay the groundwork for the more complex communications that must develop in the latter half of the first year. Here's how several parents describe their growing awareness of crying as expressive communication.

"It was confusing for me at first. Daniel was always so clear about what he wanted and when he wanted it. Andrew never was like that. I couldn't tell much from how loudly he cried or the tone. The rhythm of his crying eventually became the only way that I knew what was going on."

"I always thought that babies were hungry when they cried. It was a shock to me when I started to be able to hear cries that meant something else. Sometimes Janelle would cry as a signal that she just wanted me to talk with her from across the room. I would start to talk, and she would stop crying. If I came toward her, though, she would get more upset. At times that felt like a rejection. But she was very happy when I paid attention to her at a distance, and doing it her way also gave me more freedom to move around and enjoy myself with things that were important to me but didn't involve her. Janelle also had a shrill cry that I took to mean that she needed to be changed. Once I started watching more closely, I saw that she would often smile as soon as I walked in the room. The shrill tone was her way of getting more of my attention."

"At six weeks of age there was one cry that I could clearly identify. That was the cry that said 'Put me down,' hardly what I expected to hear since everyone told me that babies supposedly thrive on being handled. Tom would also cry for attention — but it was tentative. He was happier if I talked with him while he sat in the chair. He rarely seemed to enjoy being picked up."

"I was always scared that Michael would be in pain and I wouldn't know it. Since he required special formula, I was sure that at times his stomach must have been uncomfortable. But I also knew that my holding him would only be a distraction. He might calm for a minute, but it would not take the pain away. If the swing or the mobile made him stop crying, then he wanted something else. He was not crying because he was in pain. At first he seemed very erratic, and I couldn't always hear that the cries were different. But the arm and leg movements and the face color and expression in his eyes helped me distinguish what he was crying about until I could learn the small nuances in his voice that were also clues."

"Susan had one cry that continually stumped me. She always cried right after going to sleep. I thought that she was having nightmares — though I couldn't imagine what the nightmares of a four-week-old would be about. Maybe she was suffering in some way that I couldn't see. The thought kept me awake long into the night sometimes. I would go for a walk when she went to sleep so I wouldn't hear her crying. But if I went in there was nothing to do. She was asleep. And she did stay asleep. She stopped crying without waking up. And she still does it a year later."

"One of the greatest discoveries of the reunion of our birthing class was that I found out that two other babies were also crying when they woke up. What a relief. I was sure something was wrong with Alison. For all these babies it doesn't seem to mean anything. It's just part of the way that they wake up. Although Alison cries more on certain days. If she is tired or overexcited by what happened that day, then she cries longer and harder."

"By the time Toby was three months old I knew that he had a protest cry. He was saying 'I don't like that.' It wasn't that he was in real distress or that he couldn't handle it. Maybe he just didn't like his older sister making all of that noise, or he didn't feel like going to the neighbors to visit."

Mistakes: Learning What Is Right and Wrong

No one gets all of the messages right the first time, not even the most experienced parent. People make repeated mistakes, however, by failing to learn from their infants' behavior. Take as an example the following interchange between a five-week-old infant and his mother, which repeats itself with little variation for nearly a week. The infant, who has shut down all afternoon, wakes and immediately starts to fuss. The mother figures it's feeding time, but the baby takes half his usual intake of milk, continuing to fuss most of the time, and then forcefully vomits. After several days of this his mother decides to change her aproach. She does not feed him when the fussing begins but looks for ways to reduce the environmental and social stimulation he receives each afternoon. She concludes that the baby has not been sleeping but rather habituating as a way to reduce stress. His fusing then is an expression of fatigue, which quickly diminishes as he has less and less need to habituate. Feeding, she now understands, only increases the stimulation overload, and further agitates the baby, which explains the vomiting. Since she made the proper adjustments, the spitting stopped and he eats more.

Learning how to recognize different cries is one of the earliest phases of parent education. You must read behaviors for what they are, not what you think they should be. Parents who learn this lesson early can continue to apply it right through adolescence. The dividends are invaluable, especially for the child. Children learn from their parents. What better lesson for the child than to be judged by one's behavior and not by the ideas or the preconceptions of someone else? Here's how some parents in my practice describe their education.

"I have never been a good sleeper. Whatever time I wake up at night I almost never go back to sleep. So when Juan would wake up and cry, I always thought that he needed help to go back to sleep, and I would run right in. What a horrible thing for a two-month-old to have to stare at the ceiling all alone. But I was getting very tired, and his father was less than pleased with the whole routine. Then I began to really observe Juan's behavior when I walked into the room. He usually smiled and gurgled at me. There was no sign that he was in distress. Once I stopped going in we both did just fine."

"Sometimes with the best intentions you can set up a very confusing situation for the child. For months, every time Jane cried at night I would respond. I would nurse her. But during the day I needed her to be on a feeding schedule for my sake, and I would let her cry between times hoping that this would help her to get organized. But I came to see how very inconsistent that must seem to her. At night she got only one response regardless of what the message was; and at times during the day she got no response. No wonder she started to sleep in the daytime and be up all night. She may not have wanted to be nursed all of the time, but at least she was getting a consistent response from me and she could work with that."

"My mother had six kids and she impressed on me how important a schedule was if you were going to survive. But she only felt that she had an obligation to feed and change us at this age. To her generation, I guess, infants weren't anything more than a "lump of clay," so there was no reason to think about a baby having other primary needs. When she came to visit, she was startled to hear me say that Joseph's cry simply meant that he wanted to be talked to. She insisted that he must be hungry. I urged her just as forcefully to try my theory and talk with him. She did — for the next hour and a half! Joseph got hungry eventually, but they had a real good time together before that, and I know it was a revelation to my mother."

"One day I thought that Donnie was just pulling my leash when he started wailing, so I ignored him for a little while. When I finally went in to see if I could settle him down, I discovered that he had caught his leg in the crib slats. I felt horrible, but within a couple of seconds of being freed, he was his usual self. From then on, I could tell a distress cry from the rest, and it's the one kind of cry that brings me running, no questions asked. Thankfully, he doesn't get in a fix or hurt himself often, but it helps both of us to know that he can depend on me when he really needs me."

Finally, there is one other common "mistake" that many parents make. They respond to noises during the night that they will ignore or might not even hear during the day. Frequently the baby isn't even crying, but still they get out of bed. Usually the parents are trying to make sure that the baby goes back to sleep quickly, but this is confusing for the child. It says that you are available at night — so she is less likely to sleep or to go back to sleep if she thinks that social time is available. Remember that socializing is her most important priority. Furthermore, it twists the message system. The parents respond to a behavior cue that may not be a message for them, especially since the child isn't crying. In addition, since the response is different in the daytime, the child's world becomes more unpredictable and less trustworthy.

How Long Do You Let a Baby Cry?

Every parent asks me this question at least once. Is it two minutes, is it five minutes? Should I ever go in? The answers are maybe, maybe, and yes.

In any given instance, the answer for your child depends on three conditions:

1. Is the child trying to self-calm?

2. What's the message? — not just what does the child want, but is this a high-demand cry? Said another way, it's not just what you do, but when.

3. If you intervene, how quickly does the baby settle down, and what does his behavior tell you about your timing and what you did?

If you use the nine-step process described earlier in this chapter, or something similar, you will help yourself and the baby by providing some consistency for each of you. As you work on this for the first three, four, or six weeks, I would respond quickly to crying. Until your baby begins to self-calm, there is no point waiting. Use his responses to your interventions to learn the meaning of different cries.

But then there is a second step that occurs. It involves decisions and priorities — yours and the child's. Who will control the relationship, and how do you each maintain autonomy? Learning messages is difficult; this step is even more challenging. Does the baby who is hungry have to be fed immediately? After you spend two hours with the baby, does a cry for attention demand that you drop everything to pick the baby up? You must ask yourself difficult questions, you must compromise. You must know the cry message — what does the child want? And then you can decide what to do.

The bonus is that you get an immediate answer. You can use your child's behavior to tell you whether your response is right. If the child is trying to self-calm, then let her continue to work at it. If she is not, and you feel you must intervene, then watch her response. If she instantly settles down, or it takes only twenty seconds, then you could have waited longer. If it takes about a minute and a half to get the baby calm and reorganized, then your timing was perfect. If it takes longer than that to settle the child, then you should intervene sooner.

Fortunately, all babies can self-calm. They all are

willing to help themselves. But at the start, your baby doesn't have any ground rules. He relies on you to teach him. So, if you respond to a whimper at night, but not in the day, don't blame him for being up all night. If every time you hear a hunger cry you immediately feed him, don't blame the baby for feeling entitled to "royal service" by the time he is three months old, let alone two years old. The boundaries and the limits within the relationship start now.

In working out your own responses to crying, look for consistency, but don't carry the notion so far that you find your own needs and feelings completely subverted or ignored. At times you may be too exhausted or involved in something else, and unable to respond as you would like to. (Distress cries are the exception. Never ignore a cry that suggests your child is in pain or danger.) Your relationship with your baby is not so fragile that it cannot withstand the occasional instance in which you ignore a cry for attention. Just as your child has a cry that says "Put me down" or "Leave me alone," you the parent have an equal right to take time out once in a while. Certainly, that is preferable to feigning attention when your energy and emotions are elsewhere. The newborn can sense the ambivalence, and over the long term any child can reasonably begin to wonder whether her mother or father really cares when many of the responses are halfhearted, no matter how well intended your motives. Since children are sensitive to the intensity of a response, they will be happier with genuine responses, even if they are fewer in number, than they will be with a mix of erratic and partial efforts.

Your child will find the incentives to learn to self-calm only if he is allowed a certain amount of crying at the appropriate times. One mother said that she often thought that she was teaching her son patience. To some extent that is true, but even if the baby experiences occasional discomfort, he gains from it by learning that he can help himself by self-calming.

In the beginning you will want to choose low-stress and low-demand times to introduce your baby to self-calming. For most children, low stress means after sleep and early in the day, as opposed to late in the afternoon. What do I mean by low demand? These are situations where there is less comparative need to do something. These situations are impossible to judge unless you know the cry messages and each other's priorities. The four-week-old who is hungry and hasn't been fed for six hours is not likely to be able to calm himself. That is a high-demand cry. On the other hand, the two-month-old who is in the ninetieth percentile for height and weight and who is beginning to use his hand to self-calm, may be hungry three hours after his last feeding, but the world doesn't have to come to a stop right then in order to nurse him. He can mollify himself for a while. Another low-demand situation is the baby who protests that he wants to be held longer when you put him back in his crib after an hour in your arms. This is flattering, but the baby is being greedy. If Mother needs to take a shower, or Dad feels he should pay attention to one of the other children, this baby can be left to his own devices.

Low demand varies with the sensitivities of your child, but you will find it easier to focus first on those events that are going to be a normal part of daily existence to which the baby demonstrates some adverse reaction. For instance, my son has always been sensitive to noise. Before he could self-calm, the doorbell ringing produced instant crying. I occasionally had thoughts of disconnecting it, but he had the same reaction to the telephone ringing, and other sharp noises. He didn't like them, but he had to adapt to this intrusion, and the sooner the better. We did limit visitors to the morning, when he was more resilient. But he would still cry when the bell rang and we didn't go soothe him right away. It took a few days, but he started to find his hand to suck on. Sometimes it would take a few minutes for him to settle down, but once he got it in the morning, then he was much better in the afternoon and the telephone wasn't such a problem. Yes, you could tell from his facial expression that he didn't like the noise, but a few seconds of sucking, and he was back to his usual smiling self.

How long your child will cry when discomforted or frustrated depends on her temperament — such characteristics as persistence and intensity. The child who is highly reactive and slow to change is likely to cry for a longer time, get red in the face, sweat, even to become hysterical or vomit when confronted with the challenge of the ringing phone, and may take a long time to discover her self-calming talents. The infant who is more flexible will turn to self-calming more quickly and learn how to handle the unexpected ringing of the telephone with less difficulty. Letting your child cry for five minutes may be sufficient incentive for her to start to self-calm. For others the time will be much longer.

Be patient, and wait until you find your child's threshold. For someone as persistent as my son is, that meant waiting about fifteen minutes. But he did succeed, and so will your child. Any child can learn to do this. Even the reactive or persistent child not only can self-calm when she is crying, but can also learn to use these skills to prevent herself from getting upset.

The best index of the parents' success in this balancing act is how rapidly the child calms if the adult does intervene. If the infant calms instantly or in a very short time, say twenty or thirty seconds, then the parent could have waited longer to see if the child can pull himself together. If it does take around two minutes, then the parent is delivering the appropriate message, which can be repeated over and over again: you're available, but you are giving the child a chance to develop and use his skills to self-calm. You let him experiment and discover for himself. In one situation he may use one self-calming skill, but use a different one at another time of day or to master a different problem. The child has the incentive to self-calm, but the parent should not wait to help for so long that the baby is out of control. As he gets more secure in his ability to self-calm, then he will cry less and less. Crying will not be worth it. It will be much more enjoyable and less stressful to calm himself. He cries when he needs you to do what he can't, but otherwise he delights himself, and you, in the process.

This means timing can be used in any situation short of an outright distress cry. Just remember, if the baby is not making an effort to self-calm, *when deciding whether to wait or react, the important aspects for the parent are the message behind the cry and how quickly the child settles down if the parent has to intervene, not the actual duration of the crying itself.* The following quotes from parents of many different backgrounds and family situations illustrate how they learned about their children:

"There were times when I just couldn't tell what was going on with Gretchen or why she was crying. She would get so tense and so red in the face I thought she had to be in unbearable physical or emotional pain. But then I'd pick her up and she would instantly grin. Talk about being totally faked out — she certainly could fool me."

"I learned an important lesson about my ten-month-old the other day. Danny is a very good actor. I was making lunch when I knocked over a pan of mashed spinach. As I was cleaning up, he suddenly starts ranting and raving because he wants to be fed. I hurriedly give him a piece of bread to quiet him, but I hadn't even put it in his hand when he stopped. Quite a performance. He may have been hungry, but he wasn't that hungry. He just wanted instant service."

"Night always seems to be the hardest time to handle Charlene's crying. It is much easier to talk myself into believing that she really does need me. When Charlene had her cold she was upset, and she had a hard time sleeping through the night. I got up repeatedly to help her settle down. But after she got better, she still wanted to get up at night. Twice every night she would cry out, but as soon as I walked in, that little devil would be all smiles. She was breathing fine. She just liked having a little party at 2 A.M. So I started to wait when I'd hear her. After twenty minutes of crying I figured she must be really distraught. Wrong again. She would calm when she heard my footsteps in the hall. Her crying would be over before she even saw me. It's flattering that she enjoys my company that much. But she wasn't in distress, and when I tried waiting even longer she would put herself back to sleep."

"With James you could let him cry about something for twenty minutes and it didn't phase him. Cecelia seems more sensitive than he is, so we thought fifteen minutes of crying would be enough time for her to fall off to sleep on her own. But when we waited that long she just got more distressed and it would take a long time to calm her down. We now know that her threshold is more like eight or nine minutes. If you push her longer than that, she loses it. On the other hand, it doesn't pay to jump the gun with her. If you go in after two minutes, she acts like she expected it and makes no effort to calm herself. She was a hard case all right, but once we learned the rules, she did just fine."

Different Messages

Many, but not all, of the instances when parents have to let a child cry in the first months center around sleep and feeding times, the basics. Babies do have emotions. They do get mad, frustrated, and, certainly, demanding. As the child gets older, however, and especially as she acquires language skills, crying becomes a way to express emotions. Most notably, crying becomes an important manipulator of attention. When language fails to get the desired effect, crying has a way of persuading just about any adult to reconsider the situation and very possibly change their demands or limits on the child.

Don't do it regardless of the child's age. Parents expect this kind of manipulation from the two-year-old, but not the two-month-old. But it does happen. In each case, stick to your limits. Listen to the message and ask yourself what are the control aspects of the demand? You can always use the child's behavior, what stops the crying, to tell you how serious the situation really was. If the crying stops instantly, then the child wasn't really that upset. You may have had to respond, but you didn't have to respond right then.

Part of a parent's education to prevent this manipulation from occurring is to learn to read these emotions in the infant. These cries open new horizons as the child expands the possibilities of communication. Learning that the two-month-old can give accurate indications of what life feels like is as exciting as realizing that the two-month-old can let you know what needs to be done right then. Many of these messages come as a surprise to parents who are amazed that their child can protest so effectively or finds frustration to be a part of daily life.

Teething

All during the first year, teething is commonly cited as a principle cause of crying. This is incorrect in most cases. The vast majority of children have no trouble with teething, or they experience it as little more than an occasional nuisance. Almost never is teething the prolonged crisis that you have been warned against. Take the example of the six-month-old who has been crying and fussing continually for two weeks; in all likelihood, this is not about teeth, especially if you cannot see any teeth cutting. The crier is more likely to be demanding attention, or expressing fatigue caused by sleep problems, or relieving the frustration built up from practicing new motor skills such as crawling or sitting.

"Amy was almost five months old and she had done nothing but wail and moan for the last ten days. My mother and my neighbors tried to reassure me that it was just teething, but I couldn't see any teeth cutting. She seemed to me to be always struggling, usually trying to sit up. If I tried to help her, she would just cry harder. Meanwhile, Tylenol and the other medications I rubbed on her gums didn't work. Finally, one day she sat up on her own. You would have thought that she had just climbed Mount Everest. She was so happy that she could hardly contain it. She also stopped the wailing and moaning routine. I realized then that what I had been hearing was her frustration. She needed to sit up all right, but to do it herself, without anyone else's help. I can hardly wait until she tries walking."

"Eric was in a bad mood throughout his sixth month. I had expected that teeth would cause a problem some time around then, so I wasn't particularly surprised. On the other hand, I thought, if the problem really was teething, how come all I had to do was pick him up to quiet him? That surely couldn't make the pain go away. Besides, I could hardly afford to carry him around all day long. I got to thinking that what was going on now was a bid for attention. Maybe the vacation the month before had him rattled. On the trip he got used to having me with him all the time, and I don't think that he liked getting back to the regular routine of entertaining himself sometimes."

"Anthony was like a different kid all of a sudden. The only thing I could think of was that he was teething. None of the medications seemed to be working, and then my grandmother suggested using some whiskey. Jim brought out the best bourbon we had and I rubbed it on his gums to numb them a little. That seemed to help for a few hours, but when he woke up he looked like he had a hangover. That made me uncomfortable. Maybe the whiskey worked because we were getting Anthony drunk! But then I also remembered that I had forced him to stop taking an afternoon nap because I wanted him to sleep longer at night. That had been two days before the fussing started, and ever since his behavior had just gone downhill. Maybe he was just tired. I started to let him have his nap in the afternoon again, and he immediately got better. Two days of naps, and his teeth problems were all gone."

Separation Anxiety

Interpreting cries as an expression of separation anxiety is another common trap that can occur from a few months up through school age. This is a highly emotional issue. No mother or father wants to have a child feel abandoned every time the parents leave for work or go out for the evening. At the same time, there is something wonderful in feeling missed. Consequently, many parents react to this phase of infant behavior with mixed concern and pride. Children are often quick to pick up on the ambivalence and make good use of this powerful new tool of manipulation. And yes, separation anxiety works in reverse. The child senses that the parent needs the reinforcement of being needed constantly, and obligingly does his part to keep the parent happy. Regardless of the cause of the crying at separation, there is one point for parents to learn: *It is the child's behavior when you come together again, not the protest at separation, that can give you clues as to what the child is really protesting and how he really feels about the relationship.* Whether or not your child protests your going, his smiles at your reunion tell you what you really need to know. He's not willing to give you permission to leave, but he is happy to see you again. Control, not just protest, is part of the message. I'll let the parents in my practice tell you about these behaviors:

"I really was enjoying Anita until all of this started. Whenever I do something without her these days she starts to cry hysterically. At first I thought she was in pain, but I've come to notice that when my daughter wants to leave the room, she just crawls on out without giving it a second thought. She never even looks back, let alone protests. She certainly doesn't ask or demand that I come with her. So I have to figure that it isn't separation protest that she's displaying when she cries. She just wants me to make my moves on her terms. She has to learn that this is not the way the world works, and now's the time to get started."

"After the third day when I left Carlo at his babysitter I was beginning to think that going back to work was not a good idea. Just taking him out to the car caused the tears to start, and when I left he looked absolutely miserable. I had visions of him crying in the corner all day. But the sitter said that he stops almost as soon as I am out the door, and there is no question that he is happy to see me when I come back for him in the afternoon. He even wants me to stay there and play, and during much of that time he is preoccupied with his friends. It's pretty obvious that the protest is all for my benefit. At five o'clock he'd rather stay than come home."

"Whenever I leave, Abigail screams. I used to feel that she was terrified that I was deserting her, even though I'm not. But if you listen closely to the tone of the cry and watch her facial expression, the message is different. It has two parts. The first is that I think she is saying that she likes having me around and that she wants more. That is flattering, but leaving is not desertion. Then there's the second part — she's mad that she hasn't given her permission for this. I do have to be able to lead my own life. If I go back to her, then she stops immediately. I guess I would like to have everybody in my life behave just as I want whenever I want. Unfortunately it doesn't work that way, and I want to help her to be able to cope with the world rather than being constantly frustrated by not getting what I have led her to believe she should expect."

"It is frustrating. I put John down and he starts to cry. I feel like he won't trust me or love me if I don't go back and pick him up. But it is getting worse rather than better over the last month. It seems that I only have to think about leaving and he starts to cry. I have not been doing many things because I can't leave him. If he is developing trust then he should be getting more secure and I should be able to leave. The only thing that he is getting to trust is that I will come back. Not when I should, or when I want to, but immediately. I'm not always going to be there. He does need to be able to feel good about life and other relationships when I'm not there. Now he looks at me as some type of all-protecting umbrella. I don't think that is very healthy for him."

Stranger Anxiety

Equally challenging for many families is the question of stranger anxiety. The common interpretation is that heightened anxiety toward strangers is a sign of a strong relationship with one or both of the parents (that is, the baby doesn't want anything coming between ˙er and Mom and Dad). Rarely is this the real explanation of stranger anxiety. The secure child will usually be relaxed dealing with new people, especially as almost all of the strangers that the infant will face are trying to be positive and engaging.

But the child can react negatively to the way the unfamiliar adult approaches and handles him. As I noted in looking at social response in the chapter on communication, this has actually been going on since the baby was six or eight weeks of age. But rarely does anyone notice, even in the last half of the first year, that the child wants control over how the social interaction develops. Most especially, he does not want to be the passive victim of the stranger who deals with him without regard for his individual sensitivities. Typically, the crying is meant to protest a violation of body space, which is to say you are coming closer to the baby than the baby wants, either with insistent eye or face contact, handling, or holding. Sometimes it protests a too-loud voice, or an unfamiliar body smell to which the child's nose is highly reactive. Even parents find they must take increasing care with how they change a diaper or put on and take off a sweater as their baby gets older and more concerned with his own autonomy. No wonder then that the same small person does not want to be grabbed and jollied by a total stranger unless he invites that person to take part in some interaction.

By the time my son was five and a half months old, he had a recognizable cry for when he wanted his diaper changed. But when I put him down on his back to be changed, the cry was different. He might even stop briefly when I first picked him up. You could tell that he knew what you were going to do, and then he started that different cry because he didn't like it. Being on his back like that made him feel vulnerable — he'd kick and thrash around and his facial expression showed how he felt. For some children changing them on their stomachs eases this, but that never worked for him. He still felt out of control. As soon as I was done, and he was back in his chair, he was instantly all smiles. The balance of control was restored.

This balance of control is what stranger anxiety is really about for most children, as these parents will tell you:

"David isn't really afraid of strangers. He just likes to decide which people he wants to talk to."

"My mother could hardly wait to get her hands on Chris. She hadn't seen him for four months — then he was barely sitting and now he is walking and trying to talk. She came rushing in. He warily watched her run toward him, and started to cry when she got about five feet away from him. She picked him up and tried to console him. But he just fought even more. She tried to give him back to me, but then my phone rang and I had to go out of the room. She had to put him down on the floor. He didn't really care that I was out of sight, but he didn't want anything to do with his grandmother. Then my sister, Ann, arrived, seeming to add to the confusion. She did not notice Chris. She'd had a long flight and sat down to relax. She eventually smiled at him after he had been looking at her for a couple of minutes. My mother was still hovering over him and he was ignoring her. After a few more minutes he cruised over to Ann and offered her a toy and then wanted to be picked up by her. He had never seen Ann before in his life. He didn't have any strange reaction to her — he just wanted to do it his own way and in his own time."

"Alice really likes people. She just wants them to stay about two feet away. When we're in a store together, she will grab strangers as they walk past the grocery cart and start talking to them. They are really surprised by this ten-month-old being such a chatterbox. As long as they do not try to pick her up out of her seat or try to touch her then she keeps talking. But if they get too close she cries."

Other Cries

Children also shape crying in response to what happens around them, especially the way their parents respond. Perhaps the most common example of this is what happens when a baby or toddler falls. If each incident, regardless of the hurt, elicits a major reaction from the adult, then the child is more likely to cry and to show pain. Occasionally, the child may need help and TLC, but many falls don't hurt that much. If the parent spent less time fussing over the minor bumps and scrapes and more time enforcing limits to keep the child out of those situations that are truly dangerous, everyone would be better off.

"My daughter is truly amazing. At five and a half months she actually cries more when she hits her head if she thinks that someone is watching her. Many times she really smashes herself, but if my back is turned nothing happens. The noise is so loud I usually turn around, and she is just picking herself up, struggling to get crawling again, and going on about her business."

"Michael does fall a lot — about every five minutes. He never seems satisfied to walk; he always has to run. He rarely is hurt. He cries because he is angry that it happened or he is frustrated about his lack of success. The worst thing you can do is try to console him — he seems to take that as a signal that I think he can't do it. That really inflames his sense of injustice — it insults his independence."

While language gradually replaces crying as a favorite means of expression, the slow process of acquisition of language itself can sometimes complicate the process of you and your child trying to understand each other. Trying to learn how to communicate better is something we all struggle with, especially communicating emotions. Crying is not truly verbal. Sometimes it's a necessary outlet, but nothing can replace words.

"Casey tries so hard to make herself understood. But often times I don't seem to pick up the right cup or give her the right utensil, and then she gets angry with me and frustrated with herself. She loses control, and then starts to cry."

"Having Scott call 'Mama' at night is much harder to resist than crying. I know that it is the same old sleeping problem, to see if he can get my attention at night, but hearing 'Mama' is more difficult for me. And I know that he knows it. On the other hand, at three I can talk with him. So in the daytime I can tell him why I don't answer that at night. That part is easier now that we can talk with each other."

Language is a more flexible and more explicit medium than crying. If parents continue to overreact or overinterpret crying so that the child can use its ambiguity to her own benefit, she will do so. And she will continue to use it long after she can talk, because in crying she holds the upper hand, whereas in talking she must meet her parents as more-or-less equals.

In the preverbal child, crying is the primary means of communication. It is not just a way to express distress, nor should it automatically induce parental guilt or the feeling that every cry demands some immediate response. Parents need to be consistent and they need to have some type of predictable set of responses to determine exactly what the cries mean. As a result, they respond more accurately and reassuringly to the infant, and they understand the emotional overtones that become more and more important to maintaining family harmony.

Expressing feelings requires many outlets, including crying. Certainly the different nuances of crying may be able to show sadness, irritation, frustration, or protest, but language is far more specific and more effective, and makes the resolution of conflict much easier. Understanding emotions and how to express them helps to maintain the balance of independence and dependence that is the critical issue of growing up.

You can make crying a useful tool of communication if you follow these basic guidelines:

- Listen for the message

- Use the child's behavior to tell you whether you made the right move. The baby who will not feed isn't hungry; the child who smiles when you walk in the room wants attention; the infant who has a tantrum when you walk out the door, but gleefully dashes out of the room in his walker wants total control; the child who screams when the babysitter arrives, but goes back to playing when you leave is putting on an act.

- Babies always cry for a reason. No one wastes energy. What is your baby trying to say? In the first weeks concentrate on learning the messages. Then listen harder for the emotional overtones and the social-control inflections, which are as important as the message itself.

- Trust and communication are built on the mutual expectation of the appropriate response for that message. Doing more is not best for you or your baby.

CHAPTER 6

Self-Calming

In this chapter I'll explain what your infant can do to self-calm and the techniques you can use to help him learn specific skills. The emphasis in self-calming is on self. The parents don't feed, rock, talk, walk or give their child a pacifier: *the baby settles herself down without assistance from anyone.*

Numerous research publications in the last decade have indicated that newborns who become calmed by being in a certain body position can even tolerate painful medical procedures more easily. Think what your baby can do for himself at home! As his ability to self-calm improves, a child can prevent himself from getting upset in situations where he used to cry. Eventually, he can use these skills to gain greater self-control and begin to entertain himself.

Self-calming creates greater self-assurance and self-sufficiency. Rather than being a helpless baby, your child can finally do something for herself. She feels a sense of accomplishment and is far less vulnerable, because she is less dependent on other people. On the other hand, the child who has no independent calming skills will be angry and frightened because she feels abandoned at those times when parents, inevitably, can't be there to rescue her.

For parents, the baby's self-calming skill is equally indispensable. It provides a level of comfort and flexibility that parents cannot create on their own. Children who self-calm sleep longer at night, nap at predictable times, travel better, feed more consistently, and are socially more responsive. In short, these children are more enjoyable and less burdensome.

Habituation: Shut Down and Shut Off

During the first few weeks many parents fail to see the need for self-calming. The baby appears to sleep for long periods of time and does not cry that often. Whenever he seems upset, feeding usually seems to solve the problem.

On the other hand, the stimulation that goes with living in most households, even those designed with a baby in mind, is too much. The peace and quiet is dependent on habituation: The baby can shut down when the level of stimulation becomes uncomfortable, and totally shut off for hours if the situation is intolerable.

Some newborns, however, are never very good at habituation, and by two or three months of age few infants can still shut down; almost none can shut off. Then, having lost these mechanisms, the infant who seemed calm and agreeable can suddenly become a screaming hellion. Like Timmy in Chapter 1, nothing seems to work to calm him down. Life changes from a blissful honeymoon to a nightmare of three-times-a-night feedings and endless fussing and crying. Eventually, most parents are motivated to change what they do with the baby.

If you find yourself in this situation, you face two choices. The first choice is to continue to respond to the crying, regardless of the time of day or night, regardless of what else is going on in your life. But remember, when you comfort in response to every whimper, your baby is controlling you, and in the long run it won't work. Total dependence is a dead end.

The second choice is to help the baby self-calm. This choice is the way to self-sufficiency and independence.

How Can I Help My Child?

Three parental skills can go a long way toward promoting your child's ability to self-calm: (1) knowing how to make your child comfortable, (2) understanding how to help your child learn a specific self-calming skill, and (3) having the courage and common sense to decide when not to intervene. *Most of all, you can help your infant and yourself by remembering that you set the stage for the baby, but your child ultimately chooses her own self-calming skills and how to perfect them.*

To make your child comfortable, start at the outset in the hospital and during the first days at home to keep the environment low-key and unintrusive. Watch the baby for cues that tell you how to adjust your behavior and the environment appropriately.

In helping your child learn specific self-calming skills, you have to be prepared to let him take the lead, but your responses and insights certainly shape the process of experimentation — what will he choose to do, and how long until he becomes good at it? As a parent you play a vital role, helping the baby become adept at a skill as well as encouraging him to try new techniques. For example, you can encourage your crying infant to try putting his hand in his mouth, so that he can suck on it. He may reject the notion instantly, or he may give up after a few unsuccessful tries, in which case he should not be forced to continue, but certainly it is worth the initial attempt. It may work; if not today, then try again tomorrow.

Be prepared also to discover whether your child is a specialist or a generalist in her methods of self-calming. For some children, one technique is a clear favorite, but this is not apparent until she has had a run at all of them. Others do quite well with any of several calming methods, separately or in combination. You may notice, for example, that while your child is most likely to put her hand in her mouth, turning her on her left side can help her calm down just as effectively — perhaps it is the body position alone, perhaps being on her left side lets her more effectively utilize vision or body motion to self-calm.

Learning when not to intervene is the third parental skill, and the most difficult. Some babies will admittedly have a hard time discovering their own self-calming talents, and in the meantime parents are sorely tempted to step in and make their struggling child feel better. But you must remember that if you are constantly applying short-term solutions to your child's crying, he will never get practice in the long-term goals of self-control. Only selective responses, based upon knowing which cries involve genuine distress and which are cries of protest, annoyance, or hunger will give you the sense of confidence and freedom to let your child discover his own abilities.

Granted, not intervening can test a parent's resolve. It's natural to want to reach over and help the baby who is having a hard time learning to suck on his hand. And perhaps she will gratefully take your finger, or a pacifier, as a substitute. But as long as your child is making any effort to work it out, no matter how sporadic the intervals of success, you should leave her alone. Sooner or later you won't be there. And if your child then has no independent skills to help herself, she will be angry and frightened because she feels abandoned.

With practice, your baby's first clumsy efforts will improve — twenty seconds of silence growing to several minutes. Within a few weeks, your child can learn to self-calm in any situation. In fact, he becomes so good a self-calmer that he learns both to self-entertain and to stop himself from getting upset at those times when he previously would have responded with frantic crying.

I have said that parents must know when not to intervene; I should also add that they must be flexible enough to reverse themselves when circumstances change. For instance, there are times when parents will want to push for and promote self-calming by letting the baby get herself back to sleep. And there are times the same parents will need to intervene when the baby wakes at night because she is ill. It is not always easy to know what to do, or when. Good judgment and constant awareness of long-term goals are ultimately the last, best test. When parents do strike this balance, if they intervene only when necessary, the family realizes another bonus of self-calming: the child develops more self-sufficiency and can more easily recover from transient regressive periods or other stressful incidents in life.

What Does My Child Do?

Self-calming is a skill system, learned through practice. Some children succeed more quickly than others, and some parents are better than others at making decisions that help their child acquire these skills.

As the infant learns to self-calm, he relies typically on *sucking, vision, and body motion or position* as his favored mode. Later, as the baby continues to develop, as new motor skills and language open new opportunities for self-calming, a child's favorite routines are likely to change. I discuss only the most common options below. Parents should be prepared to recognize and nurture whatever works best for their child at any particular time.

Sucking
In the first few months of your baby's life, sucking is likely to be the mechanism she will most frequently use to self-calm. Sucking is basically a rhythmic behavior, closely related in its rewards to rocking and foot

tapping, activities which are familiar to all of us in older children and adults. It is also a pivotal part of breast or bottle-feeding, which are widely accepted as calming activities for babies. (Much of feeding's rewards are probably in the sucking.) It doesn't matter what your child sucks on as long as it belongs to her and she's always capable of finding it for herself.

For those reasons, a pacifier won't work. It will take weeks or months before your baby can look around, find his pacifier, then reach out and put it in his mouth. Meanwhile, he needs you to keep resupplying him. And even when he has the coordination to use a pacifier, it has a way of disappearing just when you and he need it most. Indeed, it offers a wonderful opportunity for acting out when he intentionally throws it out of the crib. When you are frantically searching for it at 3 A.M., or when you are out in the car and you have left the pacifier at home, you will know why you want him to be self-sufficient, and why he does, too. Unlike the pacifier, or any other prop, his self-calming skills can always be depended upon, and they are never beyond reach.

When people think of babies sucking, they always talk about thumb sucking. But babies rarely start out sucking their thumbs. Most begin with the wrists, and they can start this activity even before birth, as the sucking blisters we see on the wrists of some babies in the delivery room vividly indicate. Most newborns move on to using the back of one of their hands or fists. They gradually rotate this hand position so that by eight or ten weeks of age they suck on a finger or the thumb. The quicker the infant self-calms, the sooner she opens her hand and the easier the sucking becomes. Some people worry that before a baby gets more coordinated she risks seriously damaging an eye or scratching a cornea while sucking, but I've never seen this happen, and the few minor facial-skin scratches that the newborn may inflict on herself at this stage are worth the future dividends. To be on the conservative side and to increase your comfort, you can trim fingernails, but don't inhibit your baby's efforts by pulling her hands away from her face.

Watching this skill-building process has its frustrating as well as humorous moments. Some days your baby comes so close — but doesn't quite get there. He spends more time hitting himself in the face than sucking on his hand. His antics and his effort are often touchingly funny. Other days your fondest wish will be that those twenty seconds of success could somehow last for twenty minutes, and you will be strongly tempted to do something to help him. Just keep in mind: only when he figures out how to help himself can he make progress toward self-calming.

You can encourage your baby to use sucking by following these suggestions:

- Always place your child in the body position in which she can most easily get to her hand.

- Never cover your baby's hand with mittens or sleeves.

- Trim her nails by clipping, cutting, or filing.

- Don't swaddle her; it will interfere with her ability to use sucking to self-calm.

- Help your child if she's struggling to locate her hand — but don't try to force her to take it if she starts to fight you.

As I said earlier, any parent will be tempted to intervene. It may be difficult for you initially to recognize your child's successes, and you may be tempted to rush to her rescue. But be patient — she'll get there.

The following comments from some of my patients show that your frustration and anxieties are not unique. Knowing that other parents have experienced and are experiencing emotions similar to your own may bolster your patience. These examples are also a reminder of this most important fact: if your baby isn't calming on his own, then he isn't self-calming.

Ruth is a twenty-four-year-old housewife, the mother of two children. She told me how much she had learned from her first child, Carolyn, and how that knowledge was helping her do a better job with her second daughter, Lorraine.

"It was difficult to watch Carolyn try to suck on her hand when she was six weeks old. All she got for her efforts was a punch in the eye. I can still remember her big smile when she finally got her hand; she could hardly contain her joy, even though the success only lasted for ten seconds and it took her almost three months to get there. Now, with Lorraine, I'm seeing it all very differently. At five weeks she can do more than Carolyn could at twice that age. I'm much more cautious this time. When I intervene with Lorraine, it's because I know she's really out of control — 'lost it,' as you like to say. I didn't give Carolyn enough of a chance to succeed on her own; for two months I was always rushing to help her as soon as she whimpered. But fetching the pacifier for the ten thousandth time, I realized that I had become its extension. That was degrading — hardly what I intended to be as a mother. Then I understood why you said that I was giving her a 'habit' that she was going to have to kick."

Helping your child learn to self-calm requires learning about yourself. Laurie is a thirty-two-year-old lawyer who redefined her role as mother. Part of her self-discovery was that she learned as much from her son as he did from her.

"The first three weeks were much worse than they had to be for my baby and me. You had shown me two or three times in the hospital how good Robert was with his hands, that he had a remarkable ability to suck on his wrist to keep from crying. Each time you examined him you mentioned it — how hard it was to hear his heart sounds with all the smacking going on. Even in the delivery room, he was brightest when he was sucking on his hand. But I didn't understand how important that was. Since he was my first child, I thought it was my job to make Bobby happy all of the time. I had no idea he could help himself. And the day we went home he scratched his cheek. My mother had a fit. She said that was why he cried so much, and she got me scared that he would scratch his eye. So I either swaddled him or I put his hands in the mittens that are part of the shirt sleeves. The scratch was gone the next day, but the crying didn't stop. And it continued for three weeks until our last visit, when you let him suck on his hand.

"It has taken me and Robert more than a month to get back to where he was in the nursery. After I took his hands out of the sleeves, I could instantly see the relief on his face. He stuck his hand in his mouth almost right down to his elbow, he was so excited. He kept making himself choke. But as soon as he found his hand, he was able to go without the night feedings, and his day feedings became less frequent and less frenzied. Then I had a second reaction. He wasn't a 'baby' any more. He was different because of the hand sucking. He was more independent — he didn't need me as much. What was my role as mother? It took me a while to see that sucking his thumb meant as much to me as it did to Robert. You see, his thumb got raw, so I used that as an excuse to cover his hand up again. For two days he cried and screamed, and when I uncovered his hand, he put his thumb back in his mouth and the crying stopped immediately. I think that I've finally learned the lesson. I have more free time, and I certainly sleep more. It's not what I fantasized it would be, but I think we are both happier. My biggest problem is what to do with my mother."

Ed, a twenty-nine-year-old father and landscape gardener, said this to me of his new baby daughter:

"I think that the hardest part was waiting Audrey out. By seven weeks of age she could keep herself calm most of the day. But then when I'd want her to keep calm, she couldn't. Especially if people were around, she'd get all flustered. So we had visitors in small doses.

It took about two more weeks of work. Now she sucks both hands at once and beams at everybody. She won't be picked up, though, because she finds it hard to keep sucking on her hands. One of the nicest sounds at night is to hear Audrey smacking away. It means that she'll go back to sleep OK."

Vision

Infants frequently use vision to self-calm. Even those who use sucking as their primary means of calming will almost always use vision as a kind of backup system. But exactly when and how a baby uses it can be much less obvious than with hand sucking.

The first step toward using vision as a self-calming mechanism is taken when the three- or four-week-old starts to become more adept at selecting what to look at. Having been confronted with an endless array of visual stimuli, which have no meaning to him (after all, he doesn't know that a mobile is a mobile), he begins to choose what he will focus on and what he will specifically choose to avoid.

Face-to-face interaction is very likely something he will now turn away from when he is stressed or disorganized. The reason is that social interaction, as the most attractive stimulation for the child, is also the most intense. As intense stimulation is precisely what the child in need of calming cannot tolerate, he sensibly does his best to avoid it. A white wall, or a window with a distant view, become favorite targets. You may initially think your child withdrawn or even slow because he prefers to look at objects rather than people, but rest assured it is only a passing phase. If you try to force the child to pay attention to people when he is in this mode, all you will get for your trouble is confrontation that results in crying. And if you repeatedly try to change his mind on this matter, you may actually delay by several weeks his natural inclination to elicit such contacts himself when he would otherwise be developmentally ready and eager for more social interaction.

Most infants who use sight to self-calm will find their back to be a favorite body position because it lets them see more. Turn them onto their stomachs and they cry. Any noise or talking often distracts and annoys these children. The six-week-old nurses well looking over her mother's shoulder, but if she's talked to or placed in a direct face-to-face position she will lose the sucking rhythm and stop nursing. The eight-week-old who is contentedly looking out the window may cry if she is suddenly placed in front of a mobile.

Later, as the infant becomes less overwhelmed with the intensity of the visual world, stimulating sights gradually become less disruptive and more pleasing. The three-month-old may love the mobile that he couldn't stand four weeks ago. And the child who constantly looked past you six weeks ago may actively seek face-to-face contact.

The following stories will help you to understand how your child can use vision to self-calm. Here, first, is Trudy, a twenty-six-year-old social worker:

"I was so worried for the first eight or nine weeks because Becky never sucked on her hand like my other two children did. She'd just thrash around, then suddenly stop crying and stare blankly at the wall. At times I even thought she was having a seizure. If I tried to get her attention, she'd just cry again. I admit I took it personally; after all, I'm her mother, and she's supposed to want to look at me. It hurt that she was more interested in staring at a wall than looking at me. Finally, I realized I just had to give her some more space until she was ready. And that did it; all I had to do was let her look at the wall, she'd pull herself together, and then turn around and smile at me. I never imagined we'd end up having so much fun playing together."

Edie is a twenty-nine-year-old housewife, married for two years. She reads a lot of books and magazines about children. Her primary focus in life is her family.

"One of the most helpful things you did on our last visit was to show us that picking David up calmed him — not because he liked to be held, but because it made him open his eyes, and that gave him a chance to focus on something. When we tried it at home, he stopped crying about two thirds of the way to my shoulder, and he ended up with his head tilted back so he was looking at the ceiling. Now if I do what seems natural to me and straighten his head, he can't see what he was staring at and he starts to cry again."

For parents who are worried that they should move the baby's head because she may injure herself, she won't. Let her look at the ceiling. If you still feel you must do something, put her down in such a way, or change the position your are holding her in, so that she doesn't lose the visual target that is helping her to self-calm.

Larry is a thirty-six-year-old writer. His wife works full time, and he is the primary caregiver for their son. "Alex did better when I took down the mobile and covered the polka-dot wallpaper. That same day he fussed less and napped better. A few weeks later, as he started to take more interest in things, I took the sheets down. When he started to look at the wallpaper, I put the mobile back up."

Parents can help children who use vision to self-calm. The following suggestions will assist you in encouraging your infant's new skill:

- Put your baby down on his back or in a sitting position where he can see more easily.

- Identify his favorite visual targets and always put him in a position where he has one or more of these in view.

- Remember that a young infant will often choose to look at objects rather than people. He will more readily interact with someone if that person presents his or her face off to one side rather than full-face, and if the person does not talk at the same time.

- Keep in mind that a young infant will prefer less stimulating visual targets such as flat surfaces, single colors, lights, or windows, especially when tired. Mobiles, moving objects, busy or bold patterns, or anything that has high stimulation value is often too much for the baby to look at comfortably when he is stressed, disorganized, or fatigued.

- Recognize that picking up the child may work for many reasons — including the fact that he opens his eyes and looks at something.

- Leave a night light on if vision is the primary self-calming means that your baby uses to go back to sleep.

- Remember that noise or handling may distract and disorganize the child who is beginning to use vision to self-calm.

- Don't forget that especially late in the day, this child will often remain calmer if he is carried facing *away* from his parent's body.

- When the child becomes more interested in complex, multicolored visual items, this interest will be strongest in the morning. During the afternoon he may prefer to look at plainer, single-color objects.

Body Position and Motion

Body position is a third self-calming mechanism that many infants use. Beyond the fact that it helps certain babies to see better, and others to find a hand to suck on more easily, some infants are apparently always more comfortable in one position. Your daughter may look uncomfortable scrunched in the corner of her crib, but she got there three times in the last hour for a reason. Moving her from this position will only disturb her, and she will go back to it time and time again. Likewise, Grandmother may be convinced that her grandson's head will become misshapen from lying on his side, or that he should lie on his stomach to encourage him to crawl sooner (neither of these notions is true, by the way), but common sense says that if he likes his left side and screams in every other position, he is trying to give you a message. Pay attention to it — he wants to be on his left side and you should let him be.

Motion, or the lack of motion, may be as significant to your baby for self-calming as body position. You can only learn this by experimentation and observation. Some babies need to have their hands and arms kept free, because as they get upset or stressed, being able to "windmill" their arms keeps them from crying. Other babies don't suck on their hands but they do enjoy looking at them. Even at two or three weeks of age, they seem to concentrate on their hands and to block out everything else, thereby diminishing the stimulation load. Swaddling these infants only makes them frustrated and angry.

Still another group of babies thrive with the help of some form of containment. Left to their own devices they "windmill" their arms and legs, and this seems to get them more out of control. They get caught up in the motion, and they stop crying only when they become exhausted. As newborns these babies are markedly more content when swaddled in some way. At four to six weeks, an infant in this group will usually do better if she is simply rolled onto her stomach. She may not find her hand, but this position stops the wild motions of her arms and legs long enough for her to get herself together. Holding may not work as well as leaving her on her stomach, unless you hold her very tightly against your chest. Holding her face up, nestled in your arms, leaves her arms and legs free, and she'll start to get worked up again. The face-to-face position also presents social, visual and auditory stimulation, which may be more than she can handle. This child likes containment, but you should encourage her to provide it for herself. She may roll herself on to her stomach at an early age or simply start wrapping her arms around her chest, giving herself a hug.

Many parents feel the need to do something more with these children — the baby's awkward body motions seem to make the child's efforts appear to be a struggle. Rather than seeing the baby literally working to succeed, the parents see all that motion as a sign of failure. Just when they should let the child work it out, they intervene. If your baby is already overstimulated, this can be counterproductive, particularly if you intervene in a manner that simply adds to the child's agitation. Gentle, constant pressure on the back or soft rhythmic massage will work better than patting, the latter producing rapid staccato stimulation that generally agitates children. Patting also seems to be the universal body language to say "stop," which can only upset the baby further; he would "stop" if he could. By contrast, constant pressure or gentle massage is more soothing and gives the child an entirely different message about comfort and how you care about him.

Since the behavioral cues about body position and

body motion tend to be more difficult to read than those
for vision or sucking, parents need to be patient with
themselves and their child. If body position or body
motion helps your child to self-calm, then try the following responses:

- Let the baby's behavior tell you in what position
  she's happy, even if it looks awkward to you. If
  changing the baby's body position causes her to
  kick and scream, put her back in her original position.

- Unless you are sure that she likes to be contained,
  place your child in a position that lets her move
  her arms and legs.

- Don't force her to use sucking if she doesn't show
  any interest in her hand.

- If the baby uses body motion to self-calm, do not
  hold her tightly, because it is likely to agitate her.

- If the baby uses containment to calm, always put
  her down on her stomach unless she has the motor
  coordination to wrap her arms around her chest, a
  kind of self-swaddling.

- Ignore all of the development books that say your
  one-month-old baby can't bring her hands together
  in the middle of her body; the books are wrong.
  She may need to hold her hands in front of her
  face and look at them in order to calm down. Simply clasping her hands together may work just as
  well for her. What your baby is doing is no fluke.

• It is tempting to hold the baby who uses containment to calm down, but deciding when not to intervene enables the baby to find his own satisfactory means of containment. Remember, if you're involved, your baby isn't self-calming.

It takes time for a baby to learn to self-calm. Don't be discouraged if there are not immediate rewards. You have to learn to recognize your child's early successes and watch for the different ways he is trying to reach his goal.

This chapter has focused on the ways that infants self-calm. In the next chapter I'll discuss how long it takes and how you can help speed the process.

CHAPTER 7

The Stages of Self-Calming

It can take weeks before you recognize your baby's first attempts to self-calm, and a month more before you see success. Don't give up, and don't jump to premature conclusions of failure. Self-calming requires your baby to master a difficult new set of skills, so keep your mind open for ways to help your baby reach her goal.

The overall process has four phases: (1) an initial honeymoon phase, (2) a crisis phase, (3) a learning-and-practice phase, and (4) a final phase of perfecting and using the new skills.

Honeymoon Period

The first few weeks after birth may seem to you to be a "honeymoon period," but beneath the calm surface, a storm is brewing. New parents are often so filled with enthusiasm and so anxious to do everything right, that they don't mind getting up every two hours and walking half the night in an effort to get the baby back to sleep. Their baby also plays a part in creating the illusion of calm. His ability to *habituate* results in lengthy periods of what appears to be sleep. At this point, first-time parents rarely see the need for self-calming. Then, everything starts to wear thin, as the habituating phase comes to an end. Soon all the players, parents and baby alike, are exhausted.

Crisis

The crisis phase can arrive slowly or with a bang. Your baby may gradually sleep less during the day and fuss more, especially in the late afternoon. Or she may suddenly need to feed every two hours rather than every four and only nurse for a few minutes before falling to sleep, indicating that she is not really hungry. When you play with her, she appears jittery or anxious, and frequently explodes into extended crying. The three-week-old who a short time ago appeared to be sleeping all afternoon now wakes up crying and rarely settles down, even after feeding. As we have seen, she was not sleeping; she was, in fact, habituating.

The change in behavior can be so rapid sometimes that you may think something is physically wrong, or wonder if your parenting is off the mark. Suddenly the honeymoon is over. It seems that you spend all day doing everything for the infant. But the fact is that trying to make a baby happy all of the time, a common mistake, simply won't work.

All too often parents misinterpret what all the crying is about. They retreat to past mythology. Faced with a change that requires understanding new behaviors and making different decisions, these parents fail to experiment or react properly to the baby's behavior cues. They continue to look at the child the way our grandparents did, as passive and helpless infants. They think their baby needs extra stimulation to thrive and that is why he is crying all the time now.

By the time the baby is five or six weeks old, parents who still cannot recognize what their baby is telling them regarding stimulation can get discouraged. Mothers, especially, expend tremendous effort and endure incalculable strain to pacify the child, but the crying continues and probably even increases. Every relationship in the family is likely to suffer as a result.

What you do at this stage is critical. If you establish patterns of parent behavior designed to appease your baby, that is, if every time she cries you produce a pacifier or pick her up or try to nurse her, you will only precipitate a series of future crises. She never gains the sense of confidence and self-esteem that she can cope with the world herself, and she is always expectant, eventually demanding that you be there to help her. Inevitably her expectations will not be met. The result is colic, sleep problems, separation anxiety, stranger anxiety, and the terrible twos. On the other hand, by gently pushing her in the direction of self-calming, you are guaranteeing her a sense of independence and self-assurance.

Learning and Practice

As the protective cocoon of habituation slowly disintegrates, the parent-child relationship reaches a critical point. Now you have to make decisions. Do you see the child as independent and capable, or do you perceive him as dependent and needy? Do you want him to develop skills for dealing with life, or do you feel required to make your baby happy all of the time?

The first weeks during which a baby is learning to self-calm can be simultaneously one of the most arduous times and one of the most rewarding times for parents. You face repeated decisions that will set a pattern for how effectively you will parent. Do you understand your own priorities well enough to make decisions that will help you and your child grow toward a healthy long-term relationship, or do you use the quick fix to stop the crying for the moment? Do you strive toward developing independence for yourself and your child, or do you form a relationship scarred by crisis and dependency? Whether their child is three weeks old or three months old, parents make many decisions that affect how quickly the baby learns to self-calm and the ways in which the child actually does self-calm. The parents set the stage for the infant, and they help him achieve this goal. But the child is the one who learns the skill.

Parents who have learned the messages communicated by each of their baby's different cries (see Chapter 5) know when they should intervene and when they must let their baby try to work it out on her own. You can also increase your baby's chances of success by selecting the best times for her to start to learn these self-calming skills. Usually this is in the morning, a low-stress time when most infants are rested and have more energy available for learning new skills. Babies are less likely to succeed at learning self-calming in the afternoon. Infants who have begun to consolidate their self-calming skills will have less difficulty later in the day.

The one demand situation that parents most frequently misread is that of hunger. Because they cling to the myth that hunger is the baby's most important priority, they overlook the critical fact that feeding is a social occasion that the baby uses for sucking, body contact, motion, and other calming effects. Even though their baby was born at the fiftieth percentile for height and weight and is now at greater than the ninety-fifth percentile on weight alone, every cry gets him fed. The excuse is "Well, he's so big, he must need to eat more." Of course Mom does nothing but feed him all day — eventually every hour. And he just gets fatter. Yet the cry is very demanding, just like the cry for a pacifier becomes very demanding once the baby is hooked on that as a means to try to control his behavior. This baby uses feeding as a way to try to control his behavior, and after two or three months of building this dependency, when he can't be fed he is in a high-demand situation. Everybody else in the family is in a high-stress predicament. Rather than feeding him every hour, the parents need to change their approach. By reassessing their behavior and his, as well as their priorities and his, the real messages behind everyone's behavior become clear.

The sooner a baby learns to self-calm, the sooner the crying is restricted to high-stress, high-demand times that the baby or the infant can't be expected to cope with. The parent who realistically assesses a particular problem, determines that the child can eventually solve it for herself, and decides therefore not to intervene, can rely on the infant to keep trying until she finds the right answer.

The interim weeks require that parents maintain a sense of humor and become keen observers, appropriately setting the stage for the baby to succeed. The baby depends on you to make the right decisions about when not to intervene.

To see how the infant's skill system grows, let's look at the child who uses sucking to calm down. At four weeks of age, when for this infant habituation begins to break down, the noises of his brothers and sisters playing can make him start to cry. Watching him, we would see the following. He is lying on his left side in such a way that his hands are free. (Fortunately for him, his parents have already noticed that he seems to prefer this position, and they do their best to keep him that way. Not until he is a least three or four months old, and probably much later, will he maintain a body position on his own.) He holds his hands in tight fists and, as he fumbles for one or the other of them, he hits himself on the forehead. He cries harder. He grinds his fist into his eye, reddening it, and then clamps his mouth onto his wrist for ten seconds. Then he trembles and loses his hand and his composure. He flails and cries for twenty seconds, spits up a little milk, gets his wrist back for five seconds, and then he loses it for two minutes. His face gets red as his arms and legs windmill wildly out of control. Finally his eight-year-old sister comes over and puts the pacifier into his mouth. (She's just as prone as anyone else to seek the easy solution and meet the immediate need.)

He sucks the pacifier for three minutes, then loses it, and the minidrama begins all over again. After five minutes of fleeting successes, he finally gets his hand in his mouth long enough to fall asleep just as Mom decides that she really has to get out of the shower and rescue him.

This scenario, with variations, will happen twenty times a day, until, at six weeks, the baby will be able to get his fisted hand for twenty seconds or sometimes as long as a minute, occasionally all but choking himself in his exuberance. When he gets his hand, his body starts to relax, and he smiles. Gradually, he doesn't have to work as long at getting it, so he's not as tired, and often he will stay awake rather than falling asleep after a well-orchestrated episode.

At eight weeks of age he is even better. His fist is beginning to unfurl. Now he has other choices to make: suck on my wrist, my fingers, my thumb? Which finger or fingers? While he's not perfect at it yet, the infant has become so proficient at self-calming that no one, quite correctly, has even been tempted to give him the pacifier for a week. His older siblings make as much noise as ever, but he just sucks on his hand a little harder to compensate. He actually enjoys having the other kids around and he coos at them from time to time. He has his limits, though, and if the other children become too active or get too close, he puts his hand back in his mouth. Sometimes it takes all ten fingers to settle him down to his satisfaction.

The final move for the child who self-calms with sucking is, typically, to suck on a thumb, though an infant may prefer another finger, toes, or a wrist. As with the baby we've been watching, it usually takes weeks of experimentation to decide. Some are versatile enough to like left and right hands equally, others show passionate preferences.

There is no definite age when the practice period comes to an end; in fact, your baby actually continues to practice her first self-calming technique even as she gains other new skills. Keep in mind, however, that while she is gaining mastery, she is vulnerable to outside influences. Grandmother's weekend visit can set the process of acquiring self-calming skills back for a week or ten days if she is allowed to pick up the infant every time she cries. If you decide not to make a family fuss, you can bet that you will regret it after Grandma leaves. Similarly, if you get discouraged because you don't see enough progress and take shortcuts, for example, using a pacifier, or if you just decide you feel like being "nice" for a day, and being nice means giving in to every cry regardless of the stress level or the lack of demand, you can spoil weeks of accomplishment.

Practice takes time, usually weeks and, occasionally, months. For the infant to stay with it, parents must abide by two cardinal rules:

First, if your baby is making any attempt to self-calm, leave him alone. If he appears to need help, try to do only what is necessary to calm him enough so he can start to use his own skills to stay quiet. For example, with the four-week-old child who uses sucking effectively only on his left side, check his body position if you hear him crying, and if he can't get back to his left side on his own, move him there so that he can get comfortable again. Do not respond by picking him up or giving him the pacifier.

Second, if your baby is fussing, leave him alone. Especially from three to twelve months of age, fussing represents a twilight zone of behavior. Unlike crying, it provides no specific message. Most often, the infant is already overstimulated and fatigued, and intervening will only make things worse. The more parents do, the more wound up their baby becomes.

Self-calming is a skill system that has to be practiced. Some children are better at it than others, just as some parents are better at facilitating their child's acquisition of these skills. An occasional six-week-old infant will have five or six ways to self-calm, while others are still struggling to find one. As they get older, most children will abandon one self-calming skill, such as thumb sucking, to become proficient at a variety of others. Self-calming lets infants be flexible and resilient, abilities that enable them to cope better with all the surprises in their lives, including the antics of siblings, the anxieties of parents, and the challenges of day-care and baby-sitters.

Success: Perfecting Self-Calming

Self-calming is important to every family member, not just to parents. Even the baby's siblings appreciate it because, as their little brother or sister becomes less demanding, they get a fairer share of their parents' time. Grandparents find their visits are more pleasant. Not only is the baby social and responsive, but there are fewer fights over how to respond to cries, and no more tales of how awful the baby is for a week after they come to visit.

There are many ways to measure your child's success at self-calming. Less crying only scratches the surface. The days certainly feel different. Sleep seems a just and blissful reward. The family can enjoy an uninterrupted dinner. The child can be put down without endless crying, and mothers find that their days and nights are no longer filled by baby-care. The baby has more alert time and you begin to enjoy predictable, entertaining play time with her. You have more social time with your spouse, too. You can think about a night out, or even a vacation, without being plagued by worries of having the baby-sitter quit because the baby cried all the time. Bottom line: the fun comes back into life.

With increased alert time parent and child have an opportunity to start building their relationship. What your baby does during that alert time shows how much he has changed and how independent he has become. There is an extra twinkle, a new animation. He is more energetic and enthusiastic. As a parent, you can get involved with him in a way that was just not possible when he was crying constantly. And he in turn starts to use a new social skill: rather than just reacting to situations, he now elicits attention.

I was taught this lesson by a vivacious twenty-five-year-old gymnastics teacher named Susan. Susan had had a miserable pregnancy that climaxed with an emergency cesarean section for fetal distress. Jack, her son, came through the ordeal just fine, but during his first three weeks at home, he spent much of his time shut down. Every time Susan took Jack out for a walk, he cried continually, then fussed all night. He was difficult to nurse except in the "football" position and in a dark room. After five weeks of this, Susan was very unhappy. She had made changes to accommodate to him, but Jack had not accommodated to anything or anyone. He was making no headway with self-calming, and she was worried that another few weeks of being trapped at home would make her start to hate him.

When she called me she said she was thinking about going back to work earlier than she had planned. We talked about what was bothering her, and after I had made some suggestions as to how she could perhaps improve her situation at home, we set up an appointment for the following week. By the time her appointment rolled around, she seemed to be her animated and confident old self. She told me that after our last conversation she had started hiring a baby-sitter and going out every other morning, and that these excursions had kept her sane, but the biggest change was in Jack.

"At first he was never awake. Then he cried all of the time. When he was awake he seemed to be half there. His eyes were open, but he never seemed to be quite with it. It was almost like the habituation never wore off. Sometimes he still chooses not to respond, especially if I try to get him to pay attention to me. But most of the time when he sees me across the room, he'll motion or squeal to get my attention. And he keeps talking or smiling as long as I don't get too close. If I do, he just looks away, but he doesn't cry. When I move back, he looks at my face again. He really uses vision to help himself.

"What a tragedy it would have been if I had gone back to work early. I still have to give him a lot of space, and I wish he would play more, but there are times when he just doesn't want to, and I have to accept that I just can't make him do it. Still, there's nothing better than Jack asking for my attention — I just wait for him to start it."

Am I Being Ignored or Am I in Love?

It's unfortunate that many parents misinterpret their infant's wonderful new independence. Much of the alert time may appear strange, even undesirable, because the baby who has discovered her new powers of self-control does not automatically respond to her mother and father in the way they think she should. If, for example, she is perfectly contented sitting in a chair looking out the window, nothing else you offer her at that moment, including your own loving face, may be as attractive as what she is doing on her own. Her message is obvious: "Leave me alone for a while."

Congratulations: your baby is beginning to self-entertain. But many parents feel guilty at leaving the alert baby alone, as though they have a duty to stimulate mind and spirit at every waking moment. Your baby will tell you if she needs you. Nothing dire can happen that she cannot tell you about. To strike a livable balance, let her enjoy her new skill while you appreciate your newfound free time. This may very well be the time you really fall in love with your child.

Short Circuits

Parents sometimes convince themselves that their baby is learning to self-calm when, in reality, he is becoming dependent on something the parents are providing. Here are a few props you should avoid.

Pacifiers

True, your baby does calm down by sucking on the pacifier, but in fact neither one of you really controls the situation. Pacifiers don't give your child the psychological gratification of doing something for herself. Furthermore, as a practical matter, pacifiers simply don't work. No six-week-old can look around her crib for the pacifier, grab it, and put it back in her mouth. So at 3 P.M. or 3 A.M. when the child wakes up, you have to get the pacifier for her. But her hand is always available.

White noise

In certain situations, your child may become attuned to a certain noise, like a vacuum cleaner or fan, in order to stop crying or go to sleep. This is probably a form of habituation. Your child may appear to be "sleeping through" or be able to calm during the day as a result of this mechanical noise, but the calming effect will not last. It will fade as the ability to habituate is lost. In the late afternoon, turning on the fan may temporarily cure colic, but your baby needs to be developing better self-calming skills.

Rhythmic sounds

Rhythmic sounds are another facet of the environment that can be valuable to some infants. You may find that your baby has his own favorite music, though Mother's voice may not be an automatic calming mechanism. The fetus does hear, but newborn babies are more familiar with the sound of blood flow than anyone's voice. As is true with white noise, his reaction to these kinds of sounds gives a false impression of calming. The child may be able to use certain sounds, but he is dependent on someone else to provide it. Furthermore, your infant will lose this ability. He may still like the same sounds, but no longer will they have this magic soothing effect when he is stressed.

Mechanical swings

I call these devices "veg-o-matics." Once in the chair, an infant can seem to just tune out, or vegetate. For a short time, usually when the infant is three to twelve weeks old, the chair may appear to be a valuable aid, especially in the late afternoon. Like rocking, walking, or riding in the car, this type of repetitive motion does settle many children. But like other "short circuits," this works for only two or three months, then suddenly the child who was so consistently good turns into an inconsolable Jekyll and Hyde. The two-month-old who is spending more time in the swing chair now needs more walking or more rides in the car than she did two weeks ago. She isn't learning to self-calm, she is only getting addicted to an easy substitute.

Smell:

Smell may be very important to some infants. They often root for the breast by smell rather than touch. I have seen infants who refuse to feed, or who have major disruptions in their sleeping pattern, as the result of a parent switching their brand of soap or cologne. Any change can upset the infant's equilibrium, so if you encounter a sudden change in your child's behavior, don't overlook something as simple as a new body lotion as the reason. And you may sometimes find this was one stabilizing aspect of the environment that your child had come to depend on — just like the swing chair.

Reminders for Quick Success

1. *Believe in the process.* Your infant will discover and eventually master the self-calming skills that work best for him. On days when nothing seems to be going right, don't lose faith. It will work out. If you treat your infant as helpless and dependent, that attitude will always influence how you interpret your child's cries and how you see your baby's capabilities and potentials. Self-calming does take practice, as do most other things in life that a child and a parent must experience together.

2. *Make appropriate parenting decisions.* Parents need to understand the limits of their own capabilities. As a parent you help your child, but the last step must be hers. It's easy to put a pacifier in an infant's mouth, but this doesn't help her acquire self-calming skills. Rocking or walking may actually help the child go to sleep, but it avoids letting her learn to do it herself. Attaining the long-term goal, in this case self-calming, requires not opting for the easier, short-term solutions. Once overly protective parenting behavior is established, it becomes a pattern that can easily perpetuate itself through to adolescence, and beyond.

3. *Practice.* Self-calming is a compensating mechanism that must be practiced; it doesn't magically occur. Parents can help their child toward mastery in the following ways:

- Choose low-stress times to practice, such as the morning or right after sleep; avoid high-stress times, especially late afternoon, evening, or when your child is fatigued.

- Select low-demand times to work on self-calming skills. As you come to recognize the particular messages behind certain cries, you can more effectively choose the timing. For example, if you have just spent two hours with your child, then his demand for your attention is very flattering, but probably not very intense.

- Recognize that mastery takes time and that success will vary depending on whether your child is hungry, trying to go to sleep, or in another situation that may be stressful. As long as he continues to try to work at self-calming, let him do it.

4. *Avoid the late-afternoon crazies.* Once the infant begins to master self-calming in low-stress times, then you can start to let the child try to self-calm in more demanding situations like the late afternoon. Until that time, however, protect your child from situations that overstimulate at this time of day. Most particularly, keep her out of busy, noisy rooms like the kitchen at the end of the day.

5. *Speed up the process.* Observe your child carefully. Know what works best for him and help him to be in the right position, literally, to make maximum use of his newfound abilities.

6. *Avoid fatigue.* Tiring an infant only produces stress, and as with anyone else, the infant who is fatigued will be less able to persevere at difficult tasks. Until your baby becomes proficient at self-calming, short practice sessions work better than long ones. The infant who is fussing and overwhelmed does better if carried facing away from the parent's body, talked to in a softer voice, and held with the adult's face at an angle that avoids direct confrontation.

What's Next?

In the first two or three months, the infant who begins to feel that he can self-calm will latch on to the basic skills and then expand them, dropping some as others are attained. I continue to be amazed at the variety of self-calming skills that children find to use as they get older. The later skills are often highly individualistic, and no pediatrician can predict all the actions a given child will find to fill his very personal needs. But if you observe your youngster closely, you will see them come and go. And eventually, sometime between eighteen and twenty-four months, language will, or should, become his primary calming mechanism. It is more effective than anything else because language is a better way to express emotions. Language offers a much more efficient way to try to change a situation. He can still use all of his other self-calming skills, but language gives him the best chance of preventing being put in a stressful predicament.

CHAPTER 8

Setting a Schedule

*Making Self-Calming Work
for You and Your Baby*

"God, what a relief! I finally know how my day is going
to go. I know when I can sleep and when I can't. Nap
time may be at one or at three, but that's not important. I know that she will take a two-hour nap. I can
anticipate, roughly at least, when she'll eat, and I can't
begin to describe the bliss of being able to sleep eight
hours at night, every night." These are words that every
parent waits impatiently to be able to say. Many, sadly,
never seem to get to the promised land.

Previous generations thought that parents could and
should set the schedule because they believed that babies were helpless and compliant. Parents, especially
mothers, were made responsible for everything that the
baby did. The height of parental pride was the clockwork baby. This perfect child supposedly fed every four
hours while sleeping a minimum of ten hours at night
and napping for two hours twice a day. And of course
these events always occurred at the same time of the
day: the baby ate at 8, 12, 4, 8 and slept from 8 P.M. to

8 A.M., taking naps at 10 A.M. and 2 P.M., without a minute's variation.

If the mother was doing a good job, then it naturally followed that, when the baby struggled to resist a schedule, something such as "colic" was the cause, and once the doctor fixed that, everything would go smoothly. Doctors, who typically shared this view, were likely to "solve" the problem by prescribing paregoric or some other drug. That usually sedated the child enough to reduce the crying and fussing, after which the parents were able to impose their own schedule. But in the process the parents learned nothing about what made their child tick.

Such clockwork babies may have existed, but the forced compliance did not lead to family harmony. A schedule is a joint achievement. It serves both your needs and those of the baby. A schedule is important for everyone, but it is much more so for parents than for their baby. Nevertheless, I tell parents in my practice that setting a schedule is one of the last things you and your new baby accomplish, not the first. Until you know your child's cry messages and the other behaviors that he uses to communicate with you, and certainly until the child is able to self-calm, you cannot comfortably maintain a schedule.

What Is a Schedule?

One mother of five said that a schedule for her was when her fifth child spent more than half the day sleeping, and at least eight hours of that coincident with her own sleeping time. On the other hand, another mother with a one-and-a-half-year-old daughter said that she loved the time with her child, but valued her little girl's naps as a time for catching up with herself.

When you live with a baby, you quickly learn that a schedule does not mean that everything functions by clockwork. A schedule is not about separate decisions such as when to feed the baby or what is the best nap time. No one decision is independent of the others; there is always a circular effect. Only when you integrate these decisions do you get a schedule, that is, a set of compromises that varies from day to day, in which your self-interest doesn't always win out, but neither does the child's. In the process you discover many ways to compensate for the unexpected. Self-calming skills are the only way that your baby can compensate.

How parents and children adjust and arrive at a workable compromise varies from family to family. Since the child has no way of recognizing your priorities, you have to define the shape of the daily pattern. You can't leave it to the baby. After all, he can sleep anytime, and he doesn't have to go to work. On the other hand, his cry messages and his other forms of communication tell you what he needs and wants.

Actually, adults flatter themselves when they say they have a "schedule." We say we go to bed at 11 P.M., but it probably actually varies from ten-thirty to midnight. Just as the notions of breakfast, lunch, and dinner connote certain times of day to most adults but are not precise clock times, so, too, there are approximate times of day around which a baby comes to organize her sleeping and alert/play behavior. But the clock she watches is based on her desire for social attention and the biological needs of her body, not the timepiece on the wall. Your baby's behavior and needs will vary from day to day, in response to all kinds of internal and external events, just as yours do.

The task before you then is to work with your baby to establish a pattern that is mutually comfortable. How the baby reacts to changes in the day lets you understand him better. Your baby has all the communication skills necessary to help you work out a schedule, so don't suppress it by trying to make him fit a pattern that you think is best. Remember that most of the time you are asking him to do the unexpected, so making the baby comfortable is not just a question of what you do, but when and how you do it. Your planning gets better when you understand how you can help the baby compensate and how long the baby can calm himself when you cannot immediately respond. Yes, he can adapt — but choose the right times to ask him. You know the hunger cry that says that the baby must be fed soon; but you also know how long the baby can keep himself entertained if you would rather finish what you are doing before going to him. Likewise, naps don't occur at a fixed time. When you put the baby down is determined by your need for free time, when the baby is tired, when you may be getting tired, and, certainly, by the child's ability to self-calm.

It is this melding of self-interest, with each person at times going more than halfway to accommodate the other, which makes a livable schedule possible. For this to happen both the parent and the baby must be able to adapt. That is why self-calming is so indispensable, as the following example illustrates.

Imagine that you and your ten-week-old daughter are finally beginning to get comfortable with each other. Most days are going pretty smoothly now, though you still remember painfully the time past when she wanted to be fed every hour or two. You worried then that she was not getting enough nourishment, but you also felt secretly angry at the constant demands that left you too fatigued to do anything else. Miraculously, the problem resolved itself when she learned to suck on her hand. Almost instantly, her eating habits changed as she fed less frequently but with more enthusiasm. When she needed to calm herself, she began to turn first to her hand for help, not to you. From that time forward, she has done remarkably well at keeping herself together, and it is only occasionally, late in the day, that she seems to have trouble. When she does, you usually can distinguish between her hunger cry and her other cries for attention or comfort.

But today is different. Though each midday feeding in the last week has been almost exactly at noon, now it is only 11:25, and your baby is starting to cry. You had counted on having another half hour to yourself, and you really don't want to stop for an early feeding. Perhaps there were visitors in the morning and you need an hour to yourself to unwind from the excitement. Or maybe you are a little frantic trying to clean and cook for an important dinner party — the first time you have entertained since she was born, and for your spouse's boss, no less. You may feel pressured by your own job situation: your company has agreed to let you work at home for a while, but you know that your performance has to be better than ever to justify the unorthodox arrangement, so you are trying to turn out half again as much work as you usually do.

Whatever it is that has you wound up this morning, you resent your baby's premature cries for lunch. This was the last thing you wanted to hear. You feel deflated. What are you going to do? If you stop what you are doing and give in to her cries, then starting over will mean much more work later in the day to finish the project. You wonder, quite correctly, "Won't she be encouraged to try the same ploy again?" On the other hand, if you stick with your work, can you just let her cry for half an hour? You may reach your goal, but won't that have negative emotional consequences for both of you? She'll be angry and you'll feel guilty, so you'll all work less efficiently and she'll have a bad afternoon. But if you give in every time, then how will you ever get a schedule and how will you ever get anything done? And hasn't your mother been telling you for more than a month now that you should have her on a schedule by now, anyway? What to do?

Neither course of action works satisfactorily. It is almost impossible for any parent to let a child cry for thirty-five minutes, even when the cause is nothing more serious than an early lunch call. On the other hand, responding too readily violates something that is fundamentally important to you — your independence — and you really resent the idea of giving in. Never serving your own needs, never requiring the child to compensate, offends your sense of fairness. It feels like self-inflicted parent abuse. And it is.

So you wait, listening to her cries, for three or four excruciating minutes. You want to cry, too, only louder. You start to take your first step toward her room, dragging your conflicting emotions with you. Then the crying stops. You hesitate. You listen harder, and you can hear the sound of sucking. As you stand there, almost laughing, the memory of that great smile she had the first time she found her hand flashes across your mind. You feel better and so does she. Hurriedly, you finish whatever you were doing, glad to have held out on your own behalf. At 11:53 you go to get her, momentarily anxious that she will be angry with you for having ignored her. But she greets you with a big smile when you walk in the room. She seems just fine, and she eats a hearty meal as if to prove it.

What has happened here is that your baby has compensated for an uncomfortable feeling in her tummy by doing something to calm herself. Perhaps she has enough self-control to go on to another activity she finds entertaining. Maybe she sucks on her hand for thirty minutes. These activities won't replace food for long, of course, but it gives her some adaptability within reasonable time and discomfort limits, and that is what living within a schedule is all about.

In a society where, in a majority of families, both parents work, and at a time of life when you are starting a new role as a parent, there is too little time, not enough minutes in the day to juggle all your responsibilities unless both you and the baby can be flexible. A comfortable schedule enables you and your baby to get the most enjoyment out of being with each other. It's much better than chasing the clock.

Starting Out

Success depends on learning a very important lesson: *parents have influence, but they don't have control.* Even expectant parents sense this, even though they don't want to admit it. They justifiably worry that they are about to upset a balance involving themselves, their marriage, and their jobs that may have taken years to construct. As they see it, the new player who is joining the game doesn't know the rules, can't be reasoned with, and can't be ignored when his needs conflict with his parents' other interests. They want to maintain some stability. They want to be able to maintain a schedule so that they can plan ahead.

The best start, however, is to remain flexible. After the delivery, parents quickly discover that they can't make the child eat or sleep or smile at any given moment. But that is no reason to panic, because what you do as a parent does affect the baby. It takes most families two or three months to establish a schedule, and in the process you can learn just how competent the baby really is.

Inevitably then, in the first few weeks, there is no consistency except that of inconsistency. You as a new parent probably feel confused, but you can bet that your baby is more confused than you are. Babies are not preprogrammed to the environment that you live in. Eating dinner at six may be a habit for you, but may not be ideal for your baby. Both parents rush home from work, knowing that time together as a family is important for them and their baby, but all they find is a fussing, irritable infant who seems to want nothing to do with them. Frustrated, they try to force the child to accept them on their terms and this almost certainly causes combat.

A baby has no sense of past, present, or future. She cannot hold herself in reserve. While you know when you will get home, and look forward to seeing her as the highlight of your day, she doesn't look forward to anything. She lives in the present only, and long before you appear the three-week-old has spent everything she has trying to shield herself from the assaults of her new surroundings. She no longer has the energy or the flexibility to cope with your enthusiasm and your energy. Or else she rallies, gets tremendously enthused, but then is so "wired up" that she cannot go to sleep. In either case, you spend a tense one, two, or three hours trying to relax her, repeatedly putting her to bed only to retrieve a yelling, tense child a few minutes later. Eventually, everyone collapses in exhaustion.

It's hard to greet the morning sun after a night like that. You find yourself wondering whether parenthood is worth it and why you are such a failure as a parent. Or you entertain the idea of taking your child to the pediatrician for a checkup, since the baby who wakes at five o'clock every evening, screaming and totally inconsolable, must surely be sick.

Luckily you can avoid all this. In Chapter 3, I discussed the transition behavior that babies show when they come home from the hospital. By watching the child's behavior, you can quickly get a sense of what he likes and dislikes, of what relaxes him and what stresses him. Then you can make the necessary changes so that your baby is not so overloaded. Less stressed, he has more alert time to give to social interaction and he makes greater headway at beginning to self-calm.

The things you don't do in setting a schedule are as important as the things you do. As a start, then, try less, not more — less stimulation, less intervention, less energy. Specifically:

- Don't wake the baby.

- Don't feed by the clock — as in every four hours.

- Don't force the child to try to get accustomed to the TV, the stereo, or bright lights if his behavior says he doesn't like it.

- Don't try to make him eat.

- Don't feed him if you find that something else will work to calm him — like changing his position, which gets him to suck on his hand.

- Don't play and socialize at night, even though your baby may be more responsive and bright at 2 A.M. than at any other time of the day.

- Don't assume your child will be inherently interested in sleeping at night, as opposed to the day.

- Don't assume that you can change your baby's behavior if the same intervention wouldn't produce an identical change in your behavior. For instance, eating two dinners at night won't make you sleep better. Feeding the baby more food won't make him sleep better, either.

Fussing

Fussing, especially in the first months of a child's life, is almost always the result of overstimulation. First-time parents often misinterpret what they see, thinking it a sign that the child is bored. But to a baby, the world is anything but boring. New, incomprehensible, and unpredictable, certainly, but not boring. Parents are likely to try entertaining the fusser, but this well-meaning strategy just makes the situation worse. Instead of becoming more relaxed, the overwrought baby becomes more tense, more erratic, and more uncomfortable. And parents feel increasingly ineffective. Experienced parents know that once a child reaches this threshold of discomfort, there is no point in trying repeatedly to intervene — even if it's to do something like rocking or stroking, walking, or talking, which the child normally responds well to. The reason is that any form of interaction becomes another kind of stimulation. Possibly, she will calm a little if someone offers her a finger to suck on, but if your first try doesn't work, exhaustion may finally be the only release for the child that has gone this far.

Fussing often occurs when parents try to make the child fit into their schedule. Or it happens when they misread or ignore the signals that the infant is becoming overloaded (see Chapter 4, Communication). It even happens when you take an afternoon walk in order to relieve cabin fever. Rather than intervene, fussing is a signal to examine the day's events. What can you do differently? How can you change the sequence so the baby is more comfortable? What could you do to give the child a better chance to self-calm? Avoiding over-stimulation in the first place should be your goal.

Sleeping through the Night

Babies are not born knowing or caring about the difference between day and night. They have to be taught by the cues you give them. At night, the room should be pitch-black and your interaction with the baby as brief and dull as possible. In short, nighttime should be boring. But if everyone is lacking sleep, getting the message across clearly enough to establish a sleep-wake schedule can be a real struggle, and your baby's signals will be hard to read. Fatigue also results in the child spending more time in light sleep. The baby makes more noise, which is easy to misinterpret as crying, and is more easily awakened by normal household activities. Likewise, your signals are likely to be less consistent and predictable when you are fatigued, as you surely will be during this business of setting a schedule. It's too easy to go for the quick fix on any given night, doing whatever is necessary so that everyone can go back to sleep as fast as possible. So, as soon as you hear a peep, you jump out of bed. This gives the baby the message that you are socially available. Getting up and rocking or feeding the baby may get everyone back to sleep in a hurry, but it can cause endless future nights of sleeplessness.

For the child who must cope with a demanding environment during the daytime, night has a lot of charm. For one thing, his surroundings are subdued, mellow, and quiet. For another, his parents behave in ways that are easier for him to interact with. Tired, sleepy Mom and Dad give the kind of low-key, low-stimulus attention he wants. And because they are not so likely to be distracted by other things at this hour, they may also be a little more sensitive to his signals, a little more available. Since social interaction is the infant's highest priority, what baby given half a chance wouldn't arrange his schedule to sleep all day and be up all night?

The most common way in which parents work against their own best interests in this regard is in behaving in a way that says that feeding is more important than sleeping, when in fact their real ordering of priorities is just the opposite. Since most parents and virtually all infants use feeding as a comfort mechanism, the picture quickly becomes clouded. Before the child can self-calm, parents often use feeding as a way to get the baby to go to sleep at bedtime — thinking that it is the satiation of hunger that accomplishes this. In fact, it is the sucking, body contact, warmth, and body motion, as well as the parents' attempts to settle and calm the social environment, which are more important. Confronted with a crying baby in the middle of the night, parents tend to take the easy way out in getting the baby back to sleep. Because feeding provides so much comfort, it will often solve the problem in a hurry. But this is one short-term solution that is almost sure to produce long-term problems. Encouraged by her parents' behavior, the baby comes to expect that sleeping is always preceded by feeding, any time of the day or night. She also comes to rely on feeding as a means of comfort, quite apart from any connections with sleep.

From the baby's perspective, she can use feeding as a way to calm down or go to sleep whenever she wants. That "schedule" is fine with her. She's confused but she doesn't know it. The baby begins to get her days and nights "reversed," but with good reason.

Certainly in the first weeks, most infants have to be fed at least once during the night. But very quickly the behavior changes:

1. The pattern changes. The child who eats every three to five hours during the day wants to be fed every two hours at night.

2. The duration of the feeding changes. The baby who sucks for three minutes and falls back to sleep is giving parents a clear message. When he's hungry in the daytime he eats for fifteen or twenty minutes. Sucking for three minutes and going to sleep is a sleep mechanism. There are other variations, especially the baby who seems "uninterested" at 3 A.M. and prolongs the feeding for thirty-five minutes, but avidly nurses for ten minutes a side during the day, when he's really hungry.

3. The sucking pattern changes. As I described in Chapter 4, babies have different sucking rhythms, feeding usually being a burst-pause pattern. The baby who sucks at a slow, constant rhythm, the baby who has erratic pauses, the baby who really isn't sucking, or the baby who suddenly turns into a "barracuda," is telling you that she's not

really hungry. She may want to be up at 2 A.M., but it's not for food reasons.

4. The "demand" in the cry changes. The baby who will wait for fifteen minutes during the day to be fed can't seem to wait the twenty seconds it takes you to get to his room at night. The cry sounds like more of a crisis than just hunger, and it is, because the cry is a demand to "help me go back to sleep."

5. The social behavior changes. The baby who is generally all business about feeding in the day-time now smiles, flirts, looks around, and spends minutes just playing with the nipple. Or the baby seems half-asleep. The feeding that takes fifteen minutes in the daytime now goes on for forty minutes at night because the baby half plays, half eats.

True, the infant used to need to be fed because he was really hungry. And, yes, he's still waking up frequently at night. But once you see these changes the infant is nursing or taking a bottle solely as a calming mechanism. Remember, no baby sleeps through the night, only parents do. Even the one- or two-year-old wakes or comes into very light sleep four, five, or more times a night. The infant "sleeps through" only when he can put himself back to sleep, and for that he has to be able to self-calm.

The wise parent will work hard to turn the responsibility for sleeping through the night over to the infant. The effects are mutually reinforcing as the baby learns from your behavior and you learn from hers. As you see her late night-feeding behavior change — usually around six or eight weeks, rarely later than three months — start making yourself increasingly less available as a comforter. Your baby will continue to wake repeatedly, but she will learn to use self-calming to put herself back to sleep without any outside help.

Spoiling

As I said earlier, a schedule must be liveable. Being up half the night is not liveable. A schedule must also be a balance of differing interests. Because early patterns tend to be repeated, be aware that the balance of control established with your newborn can affect everyone's performance for years to come. This is particularly true when it comes to spoiling. Spoiling can occur at any age, even with a newborn. There are books that will tell you differently, and I certainly didn't believe spoiling was possible so young until I started hearing from parent after parent that their two-month-old was running the family. Reportedly, they were up every two hours all night long, and every time the child cried family life stopped entirely.

At first I thought there was something wrong with parents who said they were frustrated with, even mad at, their infant for behaving as though he were entitled to their attention, regardless of the time of day or night or what they were doing. Wasn't attention part of the enjoyment of this experience as well as a parental obligation? If you didn't enjoy spending time with the child, why have one in the first place?

But I was missing the point. No one can live like that. These parents, and many times the older siblings or the grandparents who lived in the same house, were simply saying that it wasn't good for them or the baby. Wistfully they would say, "Maybe he'll outgrow it," but they knew that this wasn't going to happen. Often these families might have a timetable, usually determined by the baby's feedings, but no livable schedule.

Self-calming alone will not enable families to shape a livable schedule. Parents have to identify their priorities, and sooner than I had previously realized. Now we start to talk about spoiling and what it means to them and their infant as soon as parents have learned the cry messages and the baby has started to master at least one self-calming skill. For most families this occurs when the baby is five or six weeks old.

First let's define what spoiling is. To me, spoiling occurs when the parent is:

1. Doing something that she or he does not want to do and cannot continue to do for an extended term, for example, getting up every two hours at night.

2. Doing something for the child that he can do for himself, such as rocking the child to sleep at night when he could use sucking on his own hand.

Spoiling in the case of the young infant almost always involves the parent trying to calm the child rather than letting him master the situation himself. Usually the parent is making a decision to settle a short-term problem (getting the child to go to sleep quickly at night), but the solution is almost always employed at the expense of a long-term goal (gaining proficiency in self-calming so that he can rely on himself rather than parental intervention in many demanding situations).

One visit by a doting relative who picks up your two-month-old every time she cries, regardless of what the cry message is, can erase weeks of working toward establishing a schedule. The reason is that the permissive visitor has violated your communications system. Or you may do the damage yourself when your four-month-old, who has been successfully sleeping through the night, gets a cold. You get up a couple of times a night because he is coughing and having trouble breathing. Then the cold symptoms go away. Now instead of using one of his self-calming skills to put himself back to sleep, something he had mastered nicely, he awaits your arrival. Because he was sick, he may not have been able to do this for a few nights. Going back to sleep is still difficult, even though he's no longer ill. You get up because of the cold, but he doesn't realize that. All he knows is that you got up the last three nights, so why should tonight be different? Furthermore, since your being there meets his highest priority — his need for social interaction — he is only too happy to take advantage of the situation.

So how do you break this cycle? Here is a scenario that should put you both back on track. Imagine that your baby is crying at 2 A.M. His cold is gone; he's had no symptoms for two days. You know that all you have to do is go in and let him suck on your finger for a few minutes, and he will quickly go back to sleep. You know, too, that if you wait, he will cry louder, in part because he is angry. You know he expects you to come to him. But if you do decide to go in you will never regain the schedule and the balance of control that the two of you have worked out. You wait. After twenty minutes you get out of bed wondering if maybe he's still sick, or that perhaps he has developed an earache. You open the door, and as you walk toward the crib the crying stops and you are greeted with a big grin. Your son is obviously not sick. You pick him up, smiling at his cleverness, wondering what to do now. Reminding him that this is not party time, you put him down, and leave. He protests, wanting you to stay longer.

Having been disturbed, you toss and turn for another hour, until he starts crying again. After thirty minutes you reluctantly get out of bed and start walking toward the door, just as he decides sucking on his hand is preferable to crying longer. You stand in the hall for five minutes listening to alternating bursts of sucking and fussing. Finally he goes back to sleep, and you turn back to your room and fall exhausted back into bed.

The next night, at about this same time, he starts crying, but you are determined to stick to your strategy. You notice with satisfaction that though he gets pretty wound up, he finds his hand and goes back to sleep a little more quickly this time. Night number three brings another round of crying, but before he even gets to anger he begins to suck and he's nodding off. The next night you are treated to blissful silence. By the end of the week, with no more middle-of-the-night eruptions, you are sleeping through the night and you have restored the schedule — to everybody's benefit.

Common Problems in Setting a Schedule

Since patterns in the first months do influence what happens afterward and what type of schedule you will have, I want briefly to examine some of the difficulties that you may encounter. All of these can be quickly changed by honestly looking at the priorities involved and the types of decisions being made by you and your child. The resolution always rests on the infant's ability to self-calm.

The First Days at Home

Although you desperately want a schedule so that life will feel somewhat more "normal," or back in control, accept the fact that this is not going to happen. Your baby is undergoing the most significant transition of her life, and her behavior is likely to be erratic. Trying to force her into a schedule by waking her up or making her feed every four hours will just make things more uncomfortable for her. You'll be angry and frustrated, and so will she.

Day/Night Reversal

In the first few weeks, your baby is likely to have more alert/awake time at night than during the day. This can be interpreted as a direct message that he is more comfortable when it is very dark and quiet. You can help by making it darker, quieter, and less hectic during the day. This is less draining on him, and helps him have the energy to start to learn to self-calm.

Day/night reversal also happens as a result of rigidly waking the infant to feed every three or four hours. This violates the infant's priority for sleep in preference to food. He demonstrates his position by taking very little milk and sucking only briefly. Fatigued by repeated interruptions in his sleep, he cannot get organized to go to sleep as easily and sleeps fitfully when he does. He awakens frequently, often using one- or two-minute feedings to try to go back to sleep. He is not hungry, but he is very disorganized.

Day/night reversal can also be brought on because you provide him with the best social times at night. This is especially likely to happen in the family where there are older siblings. Late at night, when there is less light, less noise, and less activity, the infant does not have to cope with as many distractions or compete with others for your attention. You are more tranquil, while still being focused on the baby. This less intense type of interaction is ideal from the infant's point of view — so he is up at night and tunes out during the day. You can help to reorganize his clock by making the daytime social environment more attractive.

Growth Spurts

From time to time your infant may go through a feeding frenzy, which is commonly labeled as a growth spurt. Usually this occurs at about one month, though it can happen at other ages. However, when measured, the infant is found not to be so much growing in length as getting fat; head circumference and length percentages do not increase as rapidly as weight. What is happening is that she is losing her ability to habituate, but because she is not yet able to self-calm, especially when she is stressed, she uses feeding as a calming activity.

Disproportionate weight gain is the principle cue that the baby is going through this phase. Others include a sucking pattern that is more frenzied, and feedings that vary from the normal pattern. Sometimes they take uncommonly long; sometimes they end much too soon with the infant falling asleep and then waking an hour later screaming, only to feed in the same intense but brief and unsatisfactory way again. Once you start to help your baby self-calm, the "growth spurt" stops dramatically. Most of these infants eventually use sucking to self-calm. Until the baby masters this self-calming skill, many parents find that in the meantime allowing the baby to suck on a finger puts a stop to feeding every hour. They let the baby suck long enough to get reorganized, so that she can eventually get her own hand. As she becomes more adept at this, they no longer have to intervene.

Catnaps

The sleeping cycles of newborns are very short, and, because they spend so much time in light sleep, they are easily disturbed by normal household occurrences. Once a child can self-calm, then he may be awakened by the same incidents, but he can put himself back to sleep.

Catnaps are common occurrences with the slightly older infant who the parent says is bored and needs to be entertained. Typically this is a ten-week-old who can only stay by himself if he is in a swing chair, or if he is moved from place to place every ten minutes. The mother who perpetuates this myth has set herself up for a schedule that insures she will never be able to get anything else done. The fact is that the infant has hardly had time to get bored with the world. But he may be unable to decide what he wants to focus on, can no longer habituate, and does not have the self-calming skills to keep himself organized so that he can provide his own entertainment. So he may nod off, but then he wakes up in a few minutes and can't get himself back to sleep. Moving him from his stomach to his back or from place to place works for a few minutes, but then he has to make another decision about what to focus on and what to do with himself.

There are also children who are particularly sensitive to some singular stimulation or occurrence. One mother of restless twins thought that her two babies were keeping each other up, but when she turned off the TV in the next room, they both napped fine. Finally, any child who is fatigued will tend to catnap instead of sleeping for two- or three-hour blocks of time. Since going to sleep, and going back to sleep, require energy and the ability to get organized, the child who is exhausted or overloaded just cannot manage. Rather than napping, she catnaps because she can't get back to deep sleep after the frequent periods when she is in light sleep. These usually occur after about ten minutes and then again thirty or forty minutes after initially going to sleep.

Sleeping in the Same Room

Sleeping in the same room with your child guarantees that neither one of you will get the sleep you need. Children do wake up at night, every night, for the first few years. Even the child who can self-calm and put himself back to sleep will make enough noise to wake you repeatedly.

To get the rest you need, you are best off sleeping in a separate room from your infant. It may seem convenient to keep the baby in your room, especially during the first weeks when you need to feed her at night. But it is not. There will be many other times during the night when the child stirs or fusses, and even her breathing may wake you. If you are in the same room, you will almost certainly be awakened repeatedly and pay the price in exhaustion the next day. And if your baby senses that you are awake, she is probably going to try to enlist your help, or better yet, demand attention before going back down.

Parents offer all kinds of reasons for why they have the child sleeping in their room, some of which can sound pretty foolish ("The wallpaper in the children's room hasn't come in yet"). The child does not care whether the decor in his room is up to snuff. Other times they will claim that having the baby by their side "is more convenient" — but as soon as they say that, I know that sleep is really not their priority. While it may take slightly less time to get the baby back to sleep if he's in their room, they are losing sleep getting up two or three times a night when they don't have to. And once up, it really doesn't matter all that much how far it is to tend the baby or how long it takes. The damage is done.

Having the baby share a room with an older sibling, is also likely to cut into your sleep. Chances are you are going to feel you have to tend the fussing baby to keep him from waking his roommate. The irony is that the older child, who sleeps more soundly than you do, rarely wakes because of the baby, but will undoubtedly do so when you come into the room. Now he also wants your attention. And the baby, meanwhile, is being encouraged to repeat the pattern again and again. Not only has he found a good way to get social time with you, he has been denied the opportunity to develop his own skills for dealing with wakefulness.

So before you get into the habit of quieting the baby, make sure that the older child's waking really is a problem. If it isn't, then just ignore the fussing for a few nights until the baby stops of her own accord. If the older child *is* being awakened regularly, then maybe the baby can sleep in another room — the dining room, the kitchen, a spare bathroom, the hall — at night until she can calm herself and settles into a less disruptive pattern. After all, the baby does not care what room she sleeps in. Self-calming, not her surroundings, is the key to everyone else in the family sleeping through and the baby being able to put herself back to deep sleep when she is in light sleep or wakes up.

The Need for Social Time

Infants do focus on what they perceive as the best social time of the day, and that is when they will try to stay awake, regardless of the actual clock time. They may be tired, but their highest priority is social interaction. So the three-month-old is just as likely as the three-year-old to refuse to go to sleep at eight if Dad always comes home at nine. Even if one of the parents has a part-time job, such as nursing three evening shifts a week, the baby may sleep fine the four nights Mom is home all evening, but regularly wake at 1 A.M. when she returns from her work. A parent in this situation is faced with a difficult decision; such behavior is very flattering, and it is tempting to do something social in response. But even a brief hello is risky if you plan to keep sleeping the other four nights of the week. Your child will turn this seemingly innocent gesture into a wonderful excuse for nightly welcome-home parties.

Feeding

Nothing causes so much disruption of a schedule, or your attempts to fashion a schedule, as waking the child up in an attempt to make him eat. Remember feeding is not his most important priority. He can tell you when he is hungry, regardless of the time of day or night. Waking him will always be negative, and the consequences regrettable.

Colic and the Arsenic Hours

Perhaps you are the parent of a one-month-old who screams every evening between five and nine, the arsenic hours. If you bottle-feed, you have probably changed her formula a few times in search of a solution. If you are nursing, you have probably been driven to drop milk products and just about every interesting food you enjoy from your diet. You have had the baby feed more often, tried to keep her awake longer, or tried to get her to sleep more in the afternoon. You have come to accept that your child has colic, but the idea of using paregoric or any other drug is anathema to everything you believe in.

But how do you find out if your baby really does have colic? Observe his behavior. The colicky baby is colicky at variable times around the clock, not just in the late afternoon and evening. Aside from having gas, he typically will have other symptoms suggesting a digestive disorder — episodes of vomiting, diarrhea, or abdominal distention. He will also be totally unpredictable in regard to when he has his best alert time. Fortunately, genuine colic is rare.

If five to nine is the time you dread, and the rest of the day is different, then your child does not have colic. But you do have a serious problem. Your child may be on a schedule of sorts, but what a schedule! You can now predict with certainty that your baby is going to drive you crazy every night at dinnertime, and nothing you do in response ever seems to work. This behavior can be changed, but the baby needs your help.

In most cases of late-afternoon "crazies," the primary problem is that the child cannot self-calm; second, she is overstimulated. By the end of the day she is simply worn out, much like the rest of us. But whereas you used to relax by running, watching TV, reading the newspaper, or having a drink on the back patio with the neighbors, your baby has no comparable way to unwind. (Chances are you're not doing too well in the relaxation department, either, these days, because now the baby cries all evening.) Therefore, she relies on you to help her with the first steps toward change. Only you can control the environment so that she does not get so overstimulated.

This means if your child is losing control at 6 P.M. every day, then from about 3 P.M. you should have him in a dark, quiet environment. You certainly don't want him out on the kitchen table while you are fixing dinner and the two other kids are noisily underfoot. Nor do you want everyone to fuss over the baby, Dad included, when they come through the door.

Other steps will help. Go out in the morning, not the afternoon. Keep the trips as brief as possible. If you have car pool responsibilities, see if you can trade off with someone else for a few weeks so that you do a few extra days when the baby is a month older and has the self-calming skills to better handle the experience. Limit the number of visitors, and let them come only if it's before lunch. Keep your older children away from the baby late in the day, even if they are not acting out in any way. The normal amount of commotion that they create may be too much for the infant. When you feed the baby in the afternoon or evening, keep social interaction to a minimum. Finally, have Dad rearrange his work schedule so that he has some relaxed time for socializing with the baby before he leaves in the morning. Father and child will both be more satisfied.

None of this is easy. It requires thinking ahead and that you reconsider many seemingly mundane situations and perhaps change them to accommodate to your baby's nature. Very likely the toughest challenges will come late in the day, when both you and your baby are least able or inclined to put in the extra effort needed to get along smoothly. I know from my own experience in dealing with my son that the things that bother a baby and put him in a desperate mood can be hard to interpret. I recall only too well being frustrated with his afternoon crying for two days running on one occasion when I was working at home. I was writing in one room with a very soft jazz tape playing at low volume while he was in another dark room a good twenty feet away. Yet he was crying so much that I couldn't get anything done, until I tried turning the tape off. I couldn't have guessed that the sound bothered him so much. I could barely hear it in the same room! But that really was the problem, and by reading his behavior and experimenting with different solutions, I eventually was able to find the answer and some peace for both of us.

If you have gotten caught in a situation where your child is overstimulated and totally out of control, you have already lost today's round. Don't drive yourself and her even more crazy by fruitlessly struggling for hours to calm her down. Every move you make to help her — more handling, rocking, talking, walking, and attempts to feed her — will only make the situation worse. Remember that the reason that she is crying is what is important, not that she is crying. The best you can do is to leave her alone in a dark, calming environment and try to figure out how you can avoid getting into this predicament tomorrow.

Removing the arsenic hours from your family's schedule requires self-calming. Many of the actions described above will help the baby be better able to self-calm. But this is a skill that he must learn for himself. While you can give him the opportunities to perfect this, only he can do it. He must decide which skills he will use and then work at them. Once he can self-calm, he is less drained by the events of the day. He becomes less vulnerable to the transitions and changes that may seem commonplace to us, but which are totally out of context for him. You can relax a little in how you plan the afternoon, and he may even become a happy participant at the dinner table instead of the screaming demon he is now. If things get to be too much, he will simply pop his hand in his mouth, look out the window, or give himself a hug. By getting himself back in control, he is no longer so dependent on you to make all of the right moves at the right time. That balance is what helps to establish the resiliency that each of us needs to cope with life. Without it there can be no predictable pattern that can be called a schedule.

A schedule is a significant family milestone — and not just because there is some tranquility back in life. Establishing a livable schedule is a major achievement, and it happens only when you discard much of the mythology that hinders many parents from being effective. It is the end result of making the right decisions, understanding each other's priorities, and successfully communicating wants and emotions.

Above all else, a schedule means that parents have been able to treat their child as a competent person with her own skills and abilities. And the infant has been able to provide the readable behavior cues and the social feedback that makes parenting possible and fulfilling. You and your baby have worked together to build a remarkable set of skills by which she can self-calm. You have become allies, not adversaries. This mutual adaptability, the predictable daily pattern called a schedule, establishes a level of comfort that is the foundation for the growth of your relationship. Many families never have the satisfaction of this type of comfort and adaptability, for one reason: you can realize a livable schedule only when your child can self-calm.

Index